I0692193

Midwest Secrets
by Maribeth Slovasky

2nd Edition 2025

Maribeth Slovasky

ISBN: 978-0-9996909-7-0

Maribeth Slovasky

To Midwesterners
everywhere.

Book One
Steel Mill Graveyard
Steubenville, Ohio

Table of Contents

Prologue

"You know, you don't have to hold my hand," said Lindsey Lesko to her Aunt Kate. Kate Popov, 24, was in Steubenville for a week, packing up the last of her things from her father's house. She was finally living her dream: getting out of Steubenville. Really, she was moving to Seattle to see if her art degree from the University of Michigan could get her noticed. She was with her niece, 8-year-old Lindsey, so her sister and brother-in-law could have some alone time. Plus, anywhere was better than Michael Popov's house. Her father and she never seemed to connect.

"I know. I know. But I promised your parents I would take care of you, and this place feels creepy when it's dark." Kate unlocked the back door of the Grand Theater, the old stage and movie house where the likes of Elvis Presley, Chubby Checker, and even old blue eyes, Frank Sinatra, performed. It's been closed for a while now, but Kate kept her key from when she worked there during high school. By then, the theater only showed movies. It was run-down; even the balcony was closed off because it was unsafe.

The backstage was pitch black, and Kate felt Linsey squeeze her hand a little tighter. Kate turned on her cellphone flashlight to see better. "I'm pretty sure the light switches are over here by the curtain operator." She walked towards the wall on their right. "Ah ha!" said Kate as she turned on the backstage lights. "Much better, huh?"

"Definitely. Okay, thanks for holding my hand. That's the darkest dark I've ever seen. the 3rd grader said as she gave her aunt a hug." I'm glad you're here, Aunt Kate. It's fun getting to be with you." Her parents, Misty and John Lesko, were in Pittsburgh for the weekend.

"We used to store the extra candy and snacks back here. Let's see if that's where they still kept them." She opened a large cabinet that was almost empty, but sure enough, there were several large boxes of chocolate candy bars, gummy snacks, licorice, even unpopped popcorn. Kate checked to see if the candy still was edible.

"Oh, yeah! How many do I get?" asked Lindsey, eyeing the selection of free snacks she was ready to devour.

"How old are you?"

"You know I'm eight. Why?"

"Then you can have nine pieces. One for each year, and one for good luck. But that's the limit, okay. Nine pieces, and no sneaking more."

"Okay, I promise. Does a whole bag of licorice sticks count as one, or do I have to open it and get how many I want?"

Kate was tapping her fingers on an old table that once was used as scenery. She was meeting Michael Buckley in the theater and was already late. "Lindsey. You may have nine bags, boxes, bars or whatever you want. They're big enough that hopefully we'll have some left for later tonight. We can't do much else but stay inside. The rain won't stop." *What a surprise.*

Lindsey was busy grabbing a Snickers Bar, a Nestle's Crunch, and looking at what else was in the cupboard. "Definitely. Can I try on some of the costumes?" There was a rack of lady's dresses and coats from different periods in history.

"Yes, but don't get them dirty or sticky. And do not tell your parents I did this! Understand?"

"KK, Aunt Kate. See ya soon."

∞∞∞

Kate walked into the theater and turned on her phone for light. "Michael are you here?" she spoke quietly.

"Last row, third seat in."

"Some things never change," she laughed as she walked to the back of the main level of the theater. Michael and Kate dated in high school, and when he came to the theater, she wouldn't sell seat C or B in Row 22. That way, she could sneak in to see him. There was never anyone in the first seat, so it was perfect for a quick kiss or a handful of Michael's popcorn. She was smiling when she sat down next to him.

"Seat B…still has the same scratches on the arms." She looked at Michael. "Hey there, how's life?"

"You look good, girl." He smiled back, leaned over and kissed her cheek. "Life is shit, to be honest. I hate this town. Can't find a real job. It sucks." Michael slouched in his chair; he looked defeated.

"So, you deal drugs to make money?" Kate was buying some marijuana from Michael. She hated Steubenville as much as he did. She left for college the day after high school graduation. The weed was to chill after Lindsey went to sleep.

6

"Shut up, Kate. I don't deal drugs. You called and asked. I'm good until my next payday, so I thought I'd share. We dated for almost a year, remember? Plus, I wanted to see you."

"You're such a sweetheart. I'm sorry. I hate this town too. I don't know why you're still here."

"I'm taking care of Pops. He has Alzheimer's. My mom won't put him in assisted living because she thinks he's gonna get better. She can't take care of him herself, so I stay. At least I have a roof and food."

"I'm sorry, Michael. I didn't know. Please give them my love." *Damn!*

"Hey, you'd do the same." He pulled out a small baggie with three rolled joints and handed it to Kate.

"Maybe, but knowing me, I'd find a way to have Misty do it. How much do I owe you?"

"No charge."

"Come on, really?" Michael nodded. "Well, then, do you have a few minutes to light one up now?" she suggested.

"Isn't Lindsey in the back of the theater?"

"Yeah, but she's eating candy and trying on costumes. I'm sure she's fine. Just a few hits. I don't want to get stoned with her around. Just relax a little." She paused and looked at Michael. "And, well, you look good too. It's nice to see someone in Steubenville outside of my asshole father." She inhaled as Michael lit the end of the joint.

She handed the joint to Michael. They sat quietly while they let the smoke fill their lungs. "Well, if you weren't babysitting, I might just have to spend $14.95 plus tax and take your pretty little ass to Motel 6. Damn hotel needs to change its name." He handed back the joint to Kate, who was laughing and trying to stay quiet at the same time.

"Motel $14.95 plus tax doesn't have much of a ring to it," she laughed again and took a deep drag from the joint. "And what makes you so certain I'd go," she said, even though she was trying to keep the smoke in her mouth. She started coughing.

"You okay?" Kate nodded. "Why? Cuz I still have that move you liked. That's why." Michael took one last hit from the joint, handed it to Kate, winked at her and walked out of the theater wiggling his still fine-looking ass.

—

Kate stepped on the end of the joint and touched it to make sure it was out completely before she put it back in the bag with the others. She sat in 22B for a few minutes, enjoying the slight buzz and thinking about Michael. She pictured them married with three kids and still living in Steubenville. She stuck her tongue out at no one, got up, and shook her

∞∞∞∞

Lindsey opened a bag of Big Red licorice and ate piece after piece, not really thinking about the candy. She had on a flapper dress and was twirling around, watching the fringe on the bottom swing as she moved. She felt very pretty and grown-up. She heard the door to the outside open, and it startled her. "Oh, Hi. What are you doing here? Aunt Kate's in the theater. She should be back any minute. I thought we were all going to see Grandpa later."

"Well, plans change honey. I like your dress. Come over here and let me see you spin in it."

"Okay. Watch."

Lindsey moved toward the lighted part of the backstage and began twirling around, laughing and humming. "I'm a flapper doing the Charleston. Can you twist me under your arms?"

"Sure. Let's dance."

"Yeah! Just don't get me wet with all the rain on your poncho. I'm not supposed to mess anything up."

The unlikely dancing team kicked their legs, and Lindsey went under the arms of her partner, laughing and making funny faces. Suddenly, she felt an arm holding her tight. Before she could say another word, a sharp knife quickly and deftly sliced Lindsey's throat. Blood was pouring from the girl's neck, and her killer grabbed a fur coat from the wardrobe rack and laid Lindsey's body on top of it.

"God, I hate the fucking mess." Still, the skillful knife handler sliced the girl's clothes down the middle, exposing her body to her knees. Then, without hesitation, the stomach, thighs, and both cheeks of the girl's buttocks were cut from her body, removing large, fleshy pieces of meat. There was an insulated bag for the girl's flesh.

The executioner used another costume, a bridal gown, to clean the knife, which was placed in the bag. Finally, the large plastic poncho, covered in blood, was removed and shoved in the bag, barely fitting.

—

"I gotta get the hell out of here before that bitch gets back." One last look around the theater and the killer was out the door.

∞∞∞∞

Kate walked backstage and called for Lindsey. She didn't see her anywhere as she began picking up the costumes Lindsey left on the ground.

"Lindsey!" she bellowed. "I told you not to make a mess. Now come over here and...Oh, my God! Oh, my fuckin' God." As Kate was picking up the wedding gown and the fur coat, she found Lindsey's lifeless body. Then she noticed the pool of blood. She looked back at Lindsey and realized her head was almost severed. When she saw the rest of what had been done to the girl, she threw up on the bridal gown, unable to comprehend what she was looking at.

With tears in her eyes, she ran outside and screamed: "Help! Someone, help!" Then, she called 9-1-1. She sat on the wet bottom step of the theater's rear entrance because she was dizzy. She was sobbing, thinking about her niece and how Misty and John were going to have to deal with their eight-year-old daughter being murdered. And mutilated. She looked up and saw Michael running towards her. She ran to him and she held him.

"What the fuck happened? I heard you screaming two blocks away. Are you okay? Where's Lindsey?"

A police siren could be heard in the distance, and Kate knew they'd be here soon. "Oh, God, Michael. It's fuckin' awful. Somehow someone got in while we were talking. She's dead, Michael. Shit! I can't believe this." More tears.

"Lindsey is dead?" he asked. She nodded. "How's that even possible? We would've heard something."

The police car came racing around the corner and pulled next to the curb, a few yards from Michael and Kate.

"Are you the one who called, Miss?"

"Yes, Jerry. I'm the one who called." Despite the horror that was happening, Kate rolled her eyes that her next-door neighbor and best friend for years, Jerry Williams, called her Miss. "It's my niece, Jer, and it's bad."

Michael walked away and let the two talk. He kept looking at the theater door, wondering what it looked like back there. He shivered. A passing car stopped when its occupants saw the police lights flashing. Monica Starling, Kate's best friend from high school, and her father walked out and saw Jerry and Kate. Monica saw Kate and went to her.

"What's goin' on?" She looked at Jerry and then Kate. "Is everything okay?"

"It's fine, Miss. We have things under control. You shouldn't be here, though. This is now a crime scene," reported Officer Williams.

"Will you please quit with the Miss shit, Jerry. My niece just got murdered!" Kate screamed at him and slapped his face. "Go do your job!" Jerry walked away, startled… and sympathetic.

Monica looked at her friend for a moment. "Murdered? Lindsey is dead?" She hugged Kate.

Michael was talking with Monica's dad when another car stopped. When Fred Lesko, Lindsey's grandfather, and Xavier Winkle, one of Fred's old friends, got out of the car, Kate dried her eyes and straightened her back. Fred moved to Columbus years ago but visited Steubenville a lot on weekends to see his son and his family. When he heard they were going to be away, he called Xavier and Fred stayed with him. Xavier owned condominiums that his brother and he converted from an old Catholic church. Monica was one of his tenants. Lindsey and Kate were going to go there after the theater, so Fred could see his granddaughter.

"What happened?" Xavier asked Monica as they walked over to the girls. "Did someone get hurt?"

"Where's Lindsey?" interrupted Fred before Monica could answer Xavier's questions. "Kate, why are you here? I thought you were coming to Xavier's. We heard on the police scanner that there was a disturbance at the theater, so we drove over. What happened? Where's my granddaughter?"

No one answered as another siren could be heard. An ambulance was racing around the corner. Kate whispered, "She's dead." And then she fainted.

Chapter 1-- Steel Mill Field Trip

Thank God this day is over. I was so tired from teaching today, I almost cussed at my students. These little 3rd graders are hellions, I swear. My name is Monica Starling, and I'm the third-grade teacher at Wells Academy in Steubenville, Ohio. Wells is the smallest of our three elementary schools, and I am the only third-grade teacher this year. I have 28 students. It's fucking crazy some days. But to split to two classes, we needed 30 students enrolled by the first day of the school year. Since that didn't happen, I got lucky and ended up with a boisterous, energetic, and quite an intelligent group of kids. I guess I shouldn't complain.

Steubenville used to be a hoppin' place. But when the steel mill closed in the 1980s, ten years before I was born, a trip to Pittsburgh on the weekend became the highlight for any kind of social life. Most of the kids I went to high school with never came back after college. I knew I'd come back. I have wanted to be a teacher since I was in 3rd grade, and I dreamed about being an elementary school teacher in Steubenville. My 3rd-grade teacher, Mrs. Morgan, was the same teacher my mother had at West Elementary. I adored her. She was always happy, always smiling, and always humming 50s music when we were working. She told us about going to see Elvis Presley in concert at The Grand in the early 60s. Now that's when Steubenville was rockin'! The closest thing we have to a rock concert is karaoke night at Banzos, a downtown bar. I wanted to be just like Mrs. Morgan.

I went to Kent State University in Northern Ohio. I loved college, but I really missed family and Steubenville. I knew what was here…really, what wasn't here. Now I live in an old Catholic church that was turned into condos about seven years ago. I live on the top floor, and the church bell is in the center of my space. My unit is the entire top floor, is circular, and has three bedrooms and two full bathrooms. I can see the Ohio River and West Virginia from my bedroom. There are two three-bedroom condos on the floor beneath me, six one and two-bedroom units on the main floor, and the contractor and landlord, Xavier Winkle, lives in the basement.

Don't think his place looks like a basement. The ladies from the church used to cook there for the priests in the parish and made pizza and fried dough every Friday to sell to the public. My family house is a half mile from the church, so Mom would give me money to get pizza for dinner on Fridays and let me have a fried dough. *Mmmm.* It was delicious. Xavier's kitchen is like a gourmet restaurant's: stainless steel counters and appliances, a brick pizza oven, a curved bar with high back chairs. The renovation was incredible. He invites his tenants down on Sundays for pizza and football. Like most of the city, he's a huge Pittsburgh Steelers fan and has a satellite so he gets every game. That's why I moved back to Steubenville: it's the people.

This is my third year with Steubenville schools. I taught my first year at West, the same elementary school I went to. I was teaching Kindergarten, and the principal knew I wasn't excited about the level. They are sweet, but to me, teaching Kindergarten was like babysitting 20 kids at once. It was more about lining up, going to the bathroom, snack time, nap time, recess--and instruction was secondary. I always felt like we never finished an academic lesson because it was time for another activity. I received a great evaluation from the principal, and I shared my enthusiasm for teaching a more academic-centered curriculum. When a third-grade position opened at Wells, my principal told me about it; even wrote me an impressive letter of recommendation. It was perfect for me.

Now I'm in the middle of my second-year teaching third grade. AND I LOVE IT. Except for one thing. The third graders from all the elementary schools take a field trip to the Wheeling-Pitt Steel Mill. It closed for good in 2005 when the Wheeling-Pittsburgh Steel Corporation went bankrupt. The field trip is the culmination of a unit of study called Making Goods USA, where we teach the kids about manufacturing, the fall of US production of goods to foreign countries who would sell at a much lower cost, and how the United States is trying to boost its manufacturing businesses again. Most of these kids are fourth, fifth, sixth generation Steubenville residents, so they know all about the mill.

My father figured he'd work at the plant like his dad, but it closed in 1979 because of the economy and foreign steel being manufactured and imported to the US. So, he worked there one year, then went to Pitt University and got an accounting degree. He figured folks would always need help with taxes, investing, and financial advice, even if there was little money for investing. We grew up in a middle-class neighborhood, and now I understand why the kids would tease me about being rich; my dad had a job and a college degree. The teasing still pisses me off.

Once the mill closed, it was just there. I remember talking to my dad about how blue the sky was. He reminded me about the smoke that was no longer billowing from the mill, the non-existent sound of the whistle that signaled the end of a shift, and the silence. No one was walking up the hill with their buddies, laughing and carrying their hard hats, Stanley lunch boxes and thermoses. The mill wasn't even boarded up. My friends would want to go there at night, claiming it was the "thing" to do. We never did. Personally, I don't think anyone ever went; just told us made up stories of things abandonment leaves behind. And last year when my class went, I was home sick with the flu, so tomorrow will be my first visit.

And for a reason I cannot explain, I'm afraid.

Chapter 2-- Not Scary at All

Since the district is small, all the third graders go to the mill together. We take buses from the school and meet at the front gate. The tour guide was my landlord, Xavier Winkle. He is nearly 80 and worked at the mill as soon as he graduated from Steubenville High School. When it closed the first time, in 1979, he began working with his brother in the construction trade. When it re-opened in the 90s, he chose not to return. I've heard him talk about how much fun working there was. He had life-long bonds with many men from his crew. Unfortunately, most of them moved away. I think that's why he has his tenants for pizza and Steelers games and does these field trip tours; he's lonely.

I figured he would keep me safe. I wish I could put my finger on what was making me so uncomfortable about the mill. There are 75 third graders, five teachers, and 14 parent chaperones. *What's to be nervous about? Hell if I know.*

"Okay, children, let's line up next to our buddy. What are the most important things to remember today?"

"Be safe, be good, and stay with your buddy!" the children shouted.

"Very good. And be courteous, listen, learn, and have fun! Are we ready?"

"Yes, Miss Starling."

The parents, students, and I walked to the gate. The two West Elementary classes were already there, and the bus from East was pulling into the parking lot. I saw Xavier, Mr. Winkle, walking toward us.

A Santa Claus-looking man slowly walked towards us. "Good morning boys and girls. Are you ready to get a little scared today?"

Some of the children looked at him with apprehension.

"Oh, I'm just kidding! No one's died in the plant for years."

Again…strange-looking faces.

"I think Mr. Winkle is just teasing, right?" I gave Xavier a pleading look.

"Of course. Boys and girls, you're in for a great day. The steel mill has been abandoned for a long time and there are some rusty machines, a lot of dirt, and a few dark and empty places. Don't worry though. We won't be going to those areas. For the most part, the history of the Wheel-Penn Steel Mill, and the story of lots of families from Steubenville lie in these now silent walls."

Thank God.

The kids from East were there now, and we followed Xavier through the gate and through a huge open metal door. The musty smell was nasty; it was damp and old mixed together. Xavier had put the lights on, and we saw how the plant looks today. One of the furnaces fell over about 15 years ago and it had been photographed by the media; CNN, *The New York Times, Men's Health, The Cleveland Plain Dealer* to name a few. That's about the most interesting event we have to brag about…a rusty furnace in an empty mill. The kids ran up to it, and Mr. Winkle told us to let them explore. The mill is open on Sunday afternoon for tours, so the city completes regular safety checks.

"Any of these kids non-natives?" Xavier asked me.

"Just Ashley Rodney from my class," I told him. Ashley and her mom live on the first floor of the church. They moved here last year, and they seem to have no visitors. I think her ex- was nasty, so she took Ashley and left. He asked the other teachers. I wondered if he had a story to tell that non-native Steubenville kids might not understand.

At the end of the building were the managers' offices and the break room. Mr. Winkle told us that a lot of the men were so disappointed on their last day at the mill that they left their personal belongings, lunch boxes, coffee cups, even a few hardhats, behind. "They felt like they'd never need them again. Some of my friends who came back after the 1979 closing never really got over it. They moved away or just kind of gave up on life."

Xavier looked down at the ground. Children are resilient and didn't understand his countenance, but I saw it…I noticed. As the children were walking away, I noticed that Xavier was looking at them carefully, especially one child I didn't know. Before he noticed me, I saw him smile, sort of. It was a bit unnerving, almost spooky.

He saw me looking, gave me the sweet old man smile I typically see and put his arm out for me. We walked together to catch up with the children.

18

"Well, I do believe we've reached the end of our tour. Does anyone have a question for me?"

"Did anyone really ever die in here, Mr. Winkle?" asked Jeremy Airato from my class.

"Not one safety accident that resulted in death, sir. That's a record we at Wheel-Penn Steubenville are very proud of. We did have a few falls and burns, but no deaths. We are the only Wheeling Pennsylvania Steel Corporation plant that can say that." Xavier smiled, his pride obvious.

"Any other questions?" After about 15 seconds of silence, Mr. Winkle thanked us for being such a great group…they were very well-behaved… and gave each child a Wheel-Penn ink pen to remember the day.

I guess I didn't have anything to be afraid of. We headed back to the busses. I wonder if I was thinking about what happened at the Grand Theater last year. A little girl from my class was found murdered, brutalized. Her, stomach, thighs, and even her butt were carved from her body. It was disgusting. *But what does the mill have to do with the theater? I don't know. Maybe it's because the little girl who died was a third grader.*

Chapter 3-- A Serial Killer…seriously

The discussion I had with my students upon our return from the mill kinda made me feel dumb for worrying. They asked good questions regarding how steel was produced, why the United States began to buy foreign-made steel, how we can work to find Steubenville some company to help all the dads who can't find work. They never cease to amaze me with their in-depth, critical thinking questions. That's the reason I love teaching third grade over kindergarten. They made the visit an important and meaningful occasion.

When I arrived home that afternoon, I knocked on Xavier's door. "Who's there?" he asked.

"It's Ms. Starling from Wells Academy, Mr. Winkle." I smiled at my answer. I usually knock, say "it's Monica," and walk in. Another reason why I love living here.

"Good afternoon, Ms. Starling," smiled Xavier as he opened his door. What can I do for you?"

"Well, for starters, let's keep it Monica. Ms. Starling makes me feel old!" We laughed.

"Come on in, Monica. I'm makin' the pizza dough for Sunday. What's up?"

"My students insisted on writing individual cards to say thank you for the great day. It really was special."

"How kind," he said, looking a little embarrassed as I handed him a stack of cards made from construction paper and various glued on ribbons and glittery trinkets. "I love doing the tours. I sure do miss that place." He browsed through the pile. "I'll read these later. Do you have time for a cup of coffee? Made the pot less than an hour ago."

"Sounds good. Do you need any help with the dough?"

"No thanks. It's rising right now. Still needs a good 30 minutes."

"May I ask a question about the mill, Xavier?"

"Sure. I thought I answered all the questions during the tour." He seemed a little surprised.

"Oh, you did. It was something I noticed. Early in the tour, you asked me if there were any students who weren't originally from Steubenville. Then later, I saw you looking at a little girl from East who didn't look the least bit familiar to me. Why so curious?"

"No reason, really. I don't know. I get kinda sad when I'm doin' the tours. I miss my friends. Most of them have moved away. Lots of them are grandparents, even great-grandparents now, so I guess I'm hoping some one's moved back to Steubenville, and their grandson or granddaughter is on the tour. That's it, really."

"Oh. Do you keep in touch with them?"

"Most yeah. We email. Still send Christmas cards, that kinda stuff. You know that little girl who was killed at the theater last year?"

"Yes. She was one of my students. It was so sad." An eerie chill went down my back.

"Well, that little girl was Fred Lesko's granddaughter. He moved to Columbus in '94, and his son, John, moved back to Steubenville in '06. I guess his wife missed home so much, his father-in-law got him a job in the city planning office. John Lesko. You know him, right?"

"I do."

Well, that little girl was their only child. I think she was a few months old when they moved back. I remember seein' her as a baby because Fred was in town to help the family get settled and we'd get together."

"Wow. I was just thinkin' about that little girl earlier today."

"Why the hell would you be thinking about that? Weren't you there that night? Yeah, with your dad? I remember Fred was visiting and we heard the 9-1-1 call on the police scanner and stopped by."

"Yes, I was there. My dad and I had dinner at La La's, and we were driving home when we saw the police. But that isn't what I was thinking about. If I tell you…promise not to laugh."

Xavier looked at me like I was crazy. "What was there to laugh at about a brutal death of an eight-year-old?" He saw the serious look on my face. "Uh…okay, I promise."

"I don't mean about the girl. I was kinda nervous about going into the mill today. Actually, I was scared."

"Why? Those third-grade tours have been goin' on for years. How can an adult be scared if they aren't?" He chuckled.

22

"I don't know! And you promised not to laugh. Some kids from high school used to tell us some pretty creepy stories of ghosts and other weird things happening there."

"And you're basing your fears off loser high schoolers who have nothing better to do than scare girls and try to get a piece. Is that it? You feel guilty because you got suckered by some horny teenage boy? Monica, it's time to grow up."

"If I did, it's not why I'm scared. Besides, that's none of your business. You'll probably tell my parents."

Now Xavier was really laughing. "What's to tell! You're almost 30 years old. What are they going to do? Ground you? Take away your cell phone?"

"I get it. You can stop laughing now. I swear I remember my dad talking about a death at the mill. Not when he was young; he only worked there for a year. I was home for Spring Break one year, and I swear he said there was a murder at the mill. Why did you tell the children no one ever died there?"

"I told them that no one ever died from working at the mill. I thought better than to share the stories about the bodies found there."

"Bodies? As in more than one?"

"Three. All children. All girls. All cut up."

The police don't like talking about it. It happened a long time ago, and they don't have a clue who did it. They interviewed the whole town. I'm surprised your dad never told you. It was messy…they were brutalized."

"Oh my God! How?"

"Like Fred's granddaughter. Parts cut out of them. The police keep it hush because the case was cold; until last year."

"I can't believe anything like that could happen in Steubenville. It's so not like us."

"Damn right. Whoever did that was smart, covered his tracks, methodically planned. Doesn't sound like anyone in this town, does it?"

"Not at all. Damn. I knew my feelings were real!"

"Don't let it get to you, Monica. Talk to your dad. He's the one smart guy in town who could explain things."

"I will. I know he does work for a lot of the guys who started up businesses after the mill closed for good. I'm sure they talk all the time."

"Good point. No wonder the police interviewed him so many times."

Chapter 4-- Daddy Knows Best

What a strange thing to say about my father. Maybe they interviewed him so many times because he's the only one with half a brain in this town!

Why am I getting pissed off? I threw my shoulder bag on the floor, kicked off my shoes, and sat on my comfy teal blue sofa and checked my cell for messages. *It's not like Xavier was being mean. He basically agreed with me without saying that most of the men in Steubenville don't have a clue, and my father is a CPA.* No messages. I texted my dad.

> Hey Dad, quick question. I vaguely remember you talking about three kids found in the mill who had been brutally murdered. Do you think their deaths are related to the one at the Grand Theater last year?

My dad is just like me; sweet and simple. Keep it to the point. Within a minute, he responded.

> Yes. Why are you asking?

> Because my landlord was the tour guide for my class field trip to the mill today, and he just mentioned the murders to me.

> In front of the kids! What an ass!

No, having coffee in his apartment.

I'd stay away from that guy, hon. He was always a creepy old man if you ask me.

You didn't say that when I moved into my condo.

Well, it's a church...used to be. And you have the best view in town.

Well, he's a sweet old man. He has his tenants over for homemade pizza and Steelers games every week.

If there are other folks around, K?

You worry too much. I'm almost 30.

Don't remind me.

My father hated to be reminded that as I got older, so did he. I smiled. *I love him so much.* I thought it was strange that my dad changed the subject from the murders at the mill to Xavier Winkle and my apartment. He's right, I have a great view!

I texted my friend Alicia and asked if she wanted to meet at La La's Diner for dinner. I'm not much for cooking and frozen stir-fry is good…just not every day. Another reason I love Xavier's pizza and game parties is the food. He makes his own secret sauce. Alicia texted back to meet at 5:00. *Maybe she remembers the murders. I hope I remember to ask.*

Chapter 5-- Unexpected Midnight Outing

Of course, we got to chatting and I forgot to ask Alicia about the murders. That night I was lying in bed and thinking about those poor children. And their parents. *Why would anyone have to experience something so heart-wrenching? Not only losing a young daughter but also knowing how they were tortured.* God, it makes me sad.

I jumped when I heard my doorbell ring. "Who is it?" It was late.

"Paul Testini, from downstairs."

I opened the door to let Paul in. We've known each other since elementary school. He's a year older and also went to Kent State. He studied accounting and was working with my father. I think he'll probably buy my dad out when he's ready to retire. Paul's a hometown guy just like me. And he's quite good-looking. I opened the door to let him in.

"Oh, that Paul Testini. I thought you were the guy I went to school with. You know, the one who works for my dad."

"Sorry, Mon. I wanted to ask you how your trip to the mill was today."

"It's almost 11 o'clock, Paul. Couldn't you wait until morning? And what do you care that my third-grade students went to the mill today?"

"Cuz I was one of the kids who was scared shitless from the stories that went around the high school. Those assholes scared the guys too." He got himself a beer, looked at me to ask if I wanted one, and sat on my recliner. "Did you see anything freaky while you were there?"

"No. Xavier was our tour guide and knows the mill inside out. He kept it age appropriate. Hey, do you remember the kids who were murdered there? It happened after the mill closed for good. There were three girls. I think it happened when we were at KSU."

"Yeah, why do you think I'm here? I know the police try to keep it quiet, but the latest tale is that the mill is haunted by three girls with mutilated bodies. I figured it was bullshit, so I thought I'd ask you if you saw anything while you were there." He had a swig of his beer.

"One, I don't think ghosts are anywhere, especially mutilated little girls in Steubenville, Ohio. And two, if they are haunting the place, I doubt they'd chase around a bunch of third graders in the middle of the day. It's never happened before, and the district has been visiting the mill for years."

"I knew you were going to say that. That's why I have a proposition for you." He paused. "Let's go out there right now. I know it's dark, but you were just there, so you should have a good sense of where we are. And we can keep our phones lit to see our way. Are you in?"

Damn him for being so hot! "And you are expecting to see?"

"Nothing, I hope. But it's been there all my life, and I've never stepped foot in it. I'm curious more than anything. Plus, it's Friday night and both of us are home alone. Says a lot about all the excitement this town has to offer."

"And what do I get out of this little adventure of yours?" I smiled, flirting just a little.

"Barbecue at Damon's Grill. I'll buy."

"You're on." *The closest thing to a date in months.* "It helps that Damon is your brother. I'll bet you get a huge discount."

"Okay. Then Damon's and breakfast at La La's."

"On two separate days?"

"Deal."

"Is this a date kind of thing?"

"Would you like it to be?"

I paused, pretending I was thinking. "Maybe. It's twice I don't have to cook."

"You might want to put something warmer on?"

I realized just then I was in my PJs…boy shorts and an old Ricky Martin tank. "Oops! I'll be right back." I heard Paul laughing as I went to my room to change. It's funny; one minute I'm flirting with a great-looking guy, and the next I'm not at all embarrassed that an old friend saw me in my Ricky Martin tank top.

We drove Paul's Jeep Wrangler to the mill. He parked it rear side in, in case we needed a quick get-a-way. We were laughing and enjoying each other's company. *I could get real used to this.* We turned off the car and turned on our cell phone flashlights.

"Ready?" I asked.

"Not really but I'm the strong, protective man now, so it's all good."

"Paul, you're an accountant. I know the type, no offense." I laughed.

"None taken, then you won't mind holding my hand?" I didn't think he was that scared and being with him made going back in the mill less frightening for me. I was happy to have a reason to hold his hand.

The delivery door was open today for the field trip, but it was closed and locked now. "What should we do?" asked Paul.

"I did see Xavier use a side door. It's probably not locked." Sure enough, the entry door to the part of the building with the lunchroom and offices opened easily. "Did you hear that?"

"What?"

"Nothing. You would think the door to an abandoned steel mill would squeak, at least a little."

"True. City Maintenance probably keeps it lubed."

I agreed. "Let's go in the lunchroom since it's right over here. The workers left a lot of their personal belongings behind. I guess they didn't want any memories of this place."

"Yet you still have your Ricky Martin shirt!"

"Go to hell, Paul. He was the love of my life!"

"Isn't he gay?"

"Thirteen-year-old girls didn't care what he was. We were Livin' la Vida Loca!"

"Time to grow up, Monica. It's the 21st century now."

"Yeah, but who was afraid of the steel mill?"

"Both of us; you just got to visit in the daylight."

"You're right. But I'm not scared now," I said as we looked around the lunchroom and picked up some coffee cups and hardhats. Someone even left a flannel shirt. It was sad.

"I'm not scared either." Paul turned to face me and touched my cheek with his hand. "Thanks for doing this, Mon. It's not the only reason I knocked on your door tonight. You aren't little Monica Starling anymore. You're beautiful." And then he kissed me.

Wow! Shivers up and down my back. Paul Testini was not only very good-looking, one small kiss in a stinky old steel mill, and I was mesmerized. I'm pretty picky. Like my dad, I'm always analyzing things. Paul's kiss left me feeling out of control…something I don't experience very often. *Wow! Wow!* I couldn't talk. Just kissed him again.

We never made it anywhere else in the mill. We drove back to the church and went to my apartment. Neither of us questioned the moment. We made love and I screamed and moaned so loud I thought I might wake a neighbor! I didn't know passion like that existed… in me especially.

∞∞∞∞

The rain was pounding on the cupola that held the church bell in my living room. The belfry was beautiful, but the rain sounded like steel drums.

"Coffee, Mr. Testini?"

"Definitely. Do you have any plans for today?"

"Lying in bed…hopefully with you."

"We are on the same page." He got up with me and ran down to his apartment to brush his teeth and grab some clothes. He didn't knock when he came in…that felt good. The day was perfect. We made love again, watched a movie, did a little work, and I felt like we were an old married couple.

"Well, Ms. Starling, may I call you my girlfriend?"

"Mr. Testini," I answered, "I do like the idea quite well. Who would have thought it?"

"Well, there's Terrence O'Neal, Tom Kolick, Sean Martini, Jimmy Bluehorn. Should I continue?"

"Stop joking."

"Monica. You have no idea how many guys thought you were hot. Still, everyone was afraid to ask you out because of your dad."

"My father! Why? He's an accountant. Oops! Sorry, I didn't mean accountants are wimps. Not all of them."

"That's twice. Anyway, we thought your father was a gangster or worked for the CIA. You had a new car when you turned 16, you lived in the nicest house in Steubenville, you wore DKNY. No one else we knew made that kind of money."

———

34

"My father is an accountant, right? I know you know how much money he makes. Why would you think he did something illegal?" I was a little pissed because I don't like thinking about my high school experience. *Maybe they thought I was hot, but they never told me that.*

"We were 17 years old, Mon. No one even knew what an accountant was, really. We just talked like that to pass the time. What else was there to do?"

"Make up stories about ghosts in the mill…and kill little girls."

"I know you don't think a local did something like that, do you? I mean, those poor little girls couldn't have been killed by someone they knew. Right?"

You're right. I don't want to think that anyone talked about my dad like that. He's such a sweetheart."

"He's one of the reasons I'm an accountant. Did you know he asked me to come to his office the Spring before I graduated high school? Knew I liked numbers and did well in math, was reliable, loved Steubenville, everything. He suggested that I major in accounting. Told me I'd have a job when I was done with college. He even helped me prep for my CPA exams."

"Wow!" *I didn't know that my dad and Paul had talked. Maybe this is meant to be.* I put my head on his chest.

"Your father is one helluva man, Monica."

"I know. And his daughter is a lucky girl," I responded.

"And his assistant is a lucky guy."

The conversation ended as we got focused on each other…again.

Chapter 6-- Letting Him In

It was Sunday and Paul and I walked down to Xavier's together. He spent Friday and Saturday night at my place, running downstairs to change, getting our mail, grabbing some wine. It was the best weekend I can remember, ever. When Xavier opened the door and saw us holding hands he smiled and said, "It's about damn time!" We laughed.

We'd eat after a 1:00 game or eat before a 4:00 game so no one had to miss anything. The Steelers were in Houston today, so dinner was first. *Thank God.* I was starving.

"Did you make your secret sauce, Xavier?" I asked.

"Of course. I just put the pizzas in the oven. They'll be done soon. I think everyone who is coming is here."

"Great. Save me a seat Paul. K? "

He kissed me. "For sure."

"Yuck." I heard Xavier say.

I always loved when we ate before a game because I'm a snacker, and I save room for chips, dessert (Marty Moran brought pies from La La's today), and my famous beef jerky. Oh yeah, I won a blue ribbon at the Ohio State Fair for my beef jerky the summer before I started high school. Been making it ever since, and I gotta say, it's gotten even better. It's the one thing I can "cook." Everyone loves it, and if I didn't want to be a teacher so badly, I could make a living selling it online. It takes almost a week to make, so I never put too much thought behind it when I was younger, especially because there wasn't really an Internet at that point, so I imagined myself on the street near Three Rivers Stadium peddling my jerky from a cart before Steelers and Pirates games. The Internet really did change the game. *Who knows what could have been?*

"Monica, what is your secret? I can't stop eating the jerky. It's so darn good," said my neighbor from the first floor, Susan Rodney, who was actually one of the few non-natives in Steubenville. She's Ashley Rodney's mom, the one who has this unknown past.

"I'll never tell, Sue. It's been my one and only secret since I was 13 years old, and I'm takin' it to the grave."

"Well, maybe Ashley and I can watch you make it. I'd love to learn. I'll close my eyes for the secret parts."

"Maybe. But it takes like a week to get it just right."

Really?"

"Yes. That, and the perfect cut of meat."

"What do you use?"

"It depends on what is available. The most important part is to get rid of as much fat as possible. That's why you rarely see jerky made from pigs. Too much fat. The meat keeps in a freezer for a long time, so I'll get extra when I find a good cut of beef."

"Well, it's delicious, Monica," said Sue, again. "It's sweet and tangy at the same time."

"Just like me!" Everyone laughed and Paul even kissed me on the cheek. There was a simultaneous "Aaawww" in the room. "What?" I asked, playing dumb.

"Looks like you might have an open condo soon," said Scott Lewis, one of the first-floor tenants and a neighbor of Paul's. "Someone might be moving upstairs."

"Chill, Scott. It's been two days," said Paul, looking a little embarrassed.

"Yeah, two days of action and more than a decade of lustin'."

"Come on, Lewis, zip it."

"Sorry, man. It's just great to see the two of you together. Monica is such a loner, and I'm sure she was crushin' on you as much as you were crushin' on her."

"Shut up!" Paul and I said at the same time. Everyone laughed and Paul put his arm around me. *Did he like me that long? What a waste of time. Oh well, there are a lot of tomorrows ahead.*

The Steelers lost but no one was too upset. They need some new blood on the field. We all said goodbye, and I walked Paul to his apartment. "I'm going to be lonely tonight."

"But we agreed. I will not be very useful if I see you naked again. And I bet your dad will read me like a book."

"I could wear my onesie flannel pajamas. That might be a turnoff."

"If Ricky Martin didn't turn me off, I doubt flannel PJs will. I don't think you understand what you do to me." He kissed me in the hallway. He started to put his hand up my shirt, and I pulled away.

"We promised. And even though I'm a good promise keeper, I know what's under your sweatshirt. I'm leaving before we both get fired tomorrow."

"You're right. This was the best weekend of my life. Even the mill was fun."

"Very," I said as I was walking away. "I'll be down at 6:00 for dinner tomorrow. With a salad and a bottle of wine."

"See you in my dreams and see you here tomorrow night at 6:00. You eat seafood, right?"

"Whatever you cook, I'm eating. See you in my dreams, too. Good night." I ran up the stairs because I was ready to go back and jump him. *My God! Paul Testini is my boyfriend!*

Chapter 7-- In a Church?

Paul and I developed a routine. He enjoys cooking; I do not, so I bought the groceries, and he cooked. Perfect. We've spent every night together for the last week, and sure enough, my dad texted me.

> Is there something going on with you and Paul?

> Why?

> Because I already know the answer and I thought my dear daughter would be happy to share her news.

> KK Yes. We kind of started dating about a week or so ago. You know he lives on the first floor of the church. We went to the mill together the same day I took the kids. One thing led to another and, well...we are a couple. What do you think?

> You aren't doing this so he'll buy me out are you?

> No dad. But thanks for putting the thought in my head that Paul is.

Paul is what?

Trying to get close to the family by dating me so he can buy you out.

Not a chance.

How do you know?

He told me he liked you when he was a senior in high school. And he already asked for my blessing to date you now, not marry you...yet.

Seriously?

Yes

And you gave it to him?

Yes, if you both promise to have dinner with Mom and me on Saturday at the house.

Of course!

Dad and Mom know? Wow! Am I ready for this? I've been on my own for so long, how am I going to have another person in my life 24/7? Shut up, Monica Starling. You lived with your parents more than half your life. You can do this.

I'm not sure why I felt I needed to give myself a pep talk. It's just that I haven't had to share my life with someone else for a long time. But if anyone is worth it, Paul is. I'm *falling in love...I think.*

∞∞∞∞

I was already in Paul's condo when I heard screaming from down the hall. I opened his door and saw Sue Rodney on the floor in the hallway, crying.

"Sue! Are you okay? Did you fall?" I ran to her side.

"No! No! My baby! Oh, God, no!" She wasn't making any sense. Just screaming and crying. I saw Xavier walking towards us.

"What's going on?" he asked.

"I don't know. I heard her screaming and found her like this." I looked down at Sue who was still on the floor.

"Susan," said Xavier. "What is the matter? Should I call for an ambulance?"

"NO!" she screamed. "No one can help her now! Oh my God, my baby!"

"Is something wrong with Ashley?" I asked.

She nodded her head. "She's inside," she said, hoarse from screaming and crying. "Don't go in there!"

——

43

"Xavier, why don't I take Sue to Paul's. Then you can check it out. Okay?" I whispered so Sue didn't hear. "Sue. Let's go to Paul's. and have some water and see if we can get you calmed down." I reached for her, and at first, she tried to pull away, but after a minute took my hand and walked with me to his unit.

What the hell happened? I got Sue a glass of water and sat down next to her on the sofa. I massaged her neck, and she calmed down a little. "Feel better?" I asked.

She looked me in the eyes, and I knew that something bad happened to Ashley. I remember when one of my students was hit by a car and was in a coma for almost a week. I saw the same look in her parent's eyes when I went to the hospital to see her. Thank God she fully recovered.

"Monica. Ashley is…dead." And the tears returned. She put her head on my shoulder and started crying again. "She's home…and…her stomach and her thighs are cut out of her precious little body. I don't know if there is more. I couldn't look at her, Monica. I left my baby alone!"

The first thing I thought about was that the killer stalking Steubenville was back again. Then I thought about Sue's husband. She hadn't said too much to me about it, but Xavier did say that he was abusive, and she had a restraining order against him. I didn't know if he saw his daughter or not.

"Sue. I'm so sorry. You didn't leave Ashley, honey. You love her. I know that. And so do you. Xavier's probably called the police already. You're where you need to be. Try to calm down. I'm sure they'll want to talk to you."

"Will you stay with me? When I talk to them?"

"Absolutely. Paul will be home in a little bit, and we'll both be by your side. And you'll spend the night upstairs with me. Is there someone I can call for you?"

Sue took a deep breath. "No, Monica. I left everyone behind to get away from Ashley's father. My parents are dead, I'm an only child, and I don't want to contact anyone who might call Anthony. That's Ashley's dad; my ex-husband. He is an evil person. Believe me."

"Do you think he had anything to do with what happened?"

"I said evil, but he's not the devil. Whatever did that to my baby is a psychopathic beast!" More tears.

We heard sirens, Xavier and Paul walked into the condo together, and Sue saw the same look on their face as I did; terror mixed with sadness. I knew Paul saw Ashley's body.

"The police are on their way," said Xavier as he walked over to the sofa and sat next to Sue. "Sue, I'm so sorry for your loss. And for the lack of security at the church." He hugged her tightly.

"Xavier, one of the reasons we moved here was because no one is supposed to worry about security. My door was locked, and Ashley knows…knew… not to let anyone in unless she knew them. She knew I would be home soon. Please don't take any responsibility for this." She hugged him, almost as if she were consoling Xavier. I teared up a little.

"You want a beer, Xavier?" Paul asked. He nodded and I hugged Paul and said I'd get them. I wanted one myself; I think we were all a bit in shock.

The next four hours flew by. The police searched for clues in Sue's unit before they removed the body. Sue asked them if she could see her face before they took her. The coroner covered the body with a clean sheet, and Paul and I went to her apartment with her. Paul stayed near the door, but I knelt beside Sue as she said her goodbyes. *Talk about sad. Wow! The woman was left with no one.*

Chapter 8-- Vigilance is a Must

The next week was a blur. Sue took a month leave of absence from the grocery store, and I took three days off work to help with funeral plans and to be there for Sue. She stayed in my guest bedroom and spent most of the time sleeping or crying. The day after the funeral, I had to go back to work, so Xavier promised he'd look in on her at my place.

On Thursday after work, I stopped at my dad's office on my way home. I missed Paul and wanted to see if he could spend the night. Sue was finally sleeping through the night, courtesy of two Tamazepam. My dad hugged me and went back in his office. He gave us privacy. That's the thing about small towns; everyone is there for each other, and Dad knew I wanted to talk to Paul alone. *God, I love him.*

"Hey, Babe. How ya doin'?" He gave me a long, wet, delicious kiss.

"I'm great now. Thanks. I needed that. I've missed you."

"Me too. I know we see each other every day, but this has been the longest week ever."

"Do you think you can spend the night?"

"With Sue there? Wouldn't that be inappropriate?" He took a step back and looked at me kind of funny.

"No. She's sleeping through the night now. She wakes up about 6:30 a.m. so you can go back to your place before then. Please. I really miss you."

"Okay, but no screaming during orgasm. Got it?"

"Oh, I only wanted to cuddle for the night. Sex? With Sue there?"

"Shit. I'm sorry. That was wrong. I thought…"

"JK. Can't wait. I'm gonna eat you up!" And with that, I kissed him on the cheek and left, laughing hysterically.

∞∞∞∞

Making love quietly isn't easy, especially when you haven't had any for a while! Paul and I texted, and he finally came up about 11:00. I wanted to be sure Sue was asleep. He was an animal, licking, biting, sucking me. "Paul, do I taste that good?"

"Mmmm," he responded while sucking on my nipple. "As good as your beef jerky."

"Yeah, but I am almost 30 years old. My meat is way too tough to use." As soon as the words came out, I regretted saying them. *Fuck. Think fast, Monica.*

"What?" He stopped and looked at me. "What butcher would sell 30-year-old meat? And are you really comparing your flesh to a cow?"

"Oh, don't go there. Maybe I need to lose a few pounds, but I'm not a cow." *Change the subject. Good idea.*

"I am not comparing you to a cow! I'm comparing your delicious tasting breast to the deliciousness of your blue-ribbon beef jerky. I'll bet you didn't know I was at the state fair when you won your blue ribbon."

"Seriously? That's funny. I was so young and inexperienced. I think I've gotten better over the years."

"Well, there's one thing I know for sure."

"What's that?"

"When I was in high school, my fantasy was to be your boyfriend and suck on your breast. And now that I'm doing both, I guarantee it's far better than I ever imagined." And back he went to sucking. I smiled. *He had no clue what he has been sucking on…and eating…through the years.*

Chapter Ate.5-- Epilogue

I got too cavalier. I thought having Sue stay at my place was genius; having her help me make beef jerky using the muscle from her daughter's thigh was going to be my most audacious act yet. But fucking asshole, Paul Testini had to get up for a drink of water in the middle of the night and found the package of meat marked Ashley R. thigh in my refrigerator. I've never made my jerky with fresh flesh and was curious to taste it and see if there was a difference.

I'd been storing my meat in an old freezer in the back of the mill for years; since the prize-winning breast meat from obnoxious Jennifer Blatone from junior high. I killed her because I couldn't stand her teasing me anymore. I cut her up to get rid of her body and decided to try to make the jerky from human meat. She was 13 when I did her; much too fatty. I may have won a blue ribbon at the state fair, but once I went younger, there was no going back. The kill was easier; all it took was an offer of candy or ice cream, and they would go anywhere with me. The muscle was so fresh and tender. Mmmm.

That's how I learned to go for the younger kids. And why I wanted to teach at Wells. The three girls at the steel mill were from East. Took forever to get all the fucking fat off the muscle when I did that. Ashley and that little bitch, Lindsey Lesko, both went to Wells. Lindsey was my student too; I thought that was bold! I did a brilliant job pretending how scared I was and how sad the deaths made me. It did get me a few weeks of great sex but really fucked up my plans.

I hate Steubenville, but there are so many dumb ass people who never would be suspicious of me. I figured it was the best place to do business. Teaching third graders made it even easier to choose my next victim. I was certain I was set for life. I knew no one ever went in the mill where I kept my stash. Living near Xavier meant I could know if anyone was snooping around in the mill. It was perfect. Then I fucked up and let my emotions think for me instead of my brain. And a little sex with a good-looking neighbor put me away for life.

As a teacher, I'll end my story with some words of wisdom: remember, boys and girls, focus on yourself, don't let anyone in, and enjoy the fruits (or shall I say meats) of your labor.

The End

Book Two

The Bizarre Bazaar

Mackinaw City, Michigan

Table of Contents

June 14 -- Preparing for the Trip

One more day and we are leaving for the summer boat trip. After 17 years, my parents finally invited me on their Lake Huron and Lake Michigan boat adventure. My dad is a priest at the Mackinaw City Episcopalian Church. He's 44 and looks 35ish. He was on the *Heavenly Lady*, our 34' Four Winns cruiser, doin' a final check. My mom's parents bought it for them as a wedding present. My grandfather is a doctor, and they are loaded.

"Dad, catch." I threw him the lifejackets, and he didn't miss one. He coached me in sports until I started high school and is as active as he was then.

"Markie, will you come on board and check the galley? Everything should be there except for the perishable food."

I took a step from the dock, and my mother held out her arm. I'm 6'3" and she's barely 5'. She weighs maybe 110 and forgets that it's me who should be helping her. I took her hand and kissed her on the cheek and said thank you. "I might have fallen in without your help."

"Shut up, Markie. I might push you in." She smacked me on my thigh, and we both laughed.

The galley looked good to go, and I checked the shelf in the head for toilet paper, soap, and shampoo. My dad yelled, "Make sure the coffee pot is there. I don't want another summer like the one when we didn't take it. Crabby people everywhere!"

I was back on deck. "Coffee pot AND coffee on board. Anything else?"

"I think we're ready," Dad smiled. We'll load the food in the morning and go. Are you ready? Do you have your journal?"

My mother is having me keep a journal of the trip to use when I write my senior thesis. "Yes." I'm not too pleased that there's schoolwork involved in this adventure.

"Aren't you excited to record your travels? What an adventure, huh?" My dad was smiling.

"You have no idea," I responded. Mackinaw City is loaded with old tourists in the summer, and the other nine months are dead. At least I have basketball at school. Our team is good, too.

My mother makes almost all the items sold at the church bazaar we have every Memorial Day weekend. Her best seller is the wind chimes she makes from fish and animal bones. They go on the boat every summer for my mom to find items to make her arts and crafts. She would be pissed if she heard me say that; she has a dual degree from Michigan State University in biology and anatomy. She fell in love and gave up a career to help Dad. What ev...

There are only two things I'm not looking forward to: skinning the dead animals she brings on board from her hunting trips and being in cramped quarters with parents...for two months.

June 15 -- Casting Off

We cast off about 10:30 from our dock at the Mackinaw marina. Two friends, James Bond and Trevor Mandy, made a Bon Voyage and Happy Hunting sign and were on the dock as we pulled out.

"Be a good boy, Marcus. Don't let your mom throw you overboard." They laughed and threw the sign on the boat as we were backing out.

"Thanks guys. I'll miss you too."

I made an inappropriate gesture, and they fell on the dock, laughing. I didn't get it until my mom walked in front of me and said, "Yes. I did see that. And yes, it's disgusting." She laughed and waved to the guys. Our family has known the Bonds and Mandys all my life. My mom took the sign and hung it in my cabin.

∞∞∞∞

We anchored somewhere near the Huron National Forest, so there was no port or dock. We were close to shore though, so I jumped in for a swim.

"Is it cold?" asked my dad.

"I'm already used to it. You comin' in?"

"I'm good." He was sitting on a lounge chair, drinking a Corona, and reading a Stephen King novel. Very priestly.

I swam a few laps around the boat, then I started feeling things touching my feet and legs. I stopped and saw a jellyfish swim by me. God, I hate these things…lake monsters.

"Grab them, Markie," I heard my mom tell me. "They're perfect for the lights I make." She saw me getting out and threw me a beach towel. "You're such a chicken. They don't bite."

"Fine. They sting. I hate when they all bunch up around my legs. It's disgusting. Thanks for the towel."

"Sure. You could have asked for the net. We haven't been out a day and you're complaining. Jellyfish are on the good side of disgusting right now. Get ready. I'm tellin' you."

"K, Mom, I get it. But I'm not picking up jellyfish. I threw the towel back to her. "I'm takin' a shower and goin' to bed.

"See you in the morning."

I heard them laughing as I went down below. We are stopping in Port Sanilac in like two days. I'm ready for a break, even if it's been less than a day. I took my shower and went to bed.

June 20 -- Port Sanilac

Port Sanilac looked even more boring than home. The old fogies were cruisin' the town and enjoying the warm early evening air. We docked early enough to eat, so the three of us had crab cakes and chips at an outside restaurant…Minnie's, I think. Then my mom went hunting while my dad and I cleaned the head, changed the water, and cleaned the Lady up a little. Dad went to a gym near the marina. He asked if I wanted to join him, but I really needed a parent break.

"I'm gonna grab a Gatorade and check things out. Thanks for the invite though. Catch ya later."

"Enjoy yourself, Markie. Ya know, a lot of teenagers come up north to work in the tourist towns for the summer. I'm just sayin'." He smiled as I rolled my eyes and left. *Good point.* I walked away not wanting to acknowledge how happy that made me.

Apparently, Port Sanilac is too far north because there were either annoying old ladies or the owners of the stores serving customers. Most of them were men who yelled at the old ladies for being too slow. I stopped at the Marina Mart, bought a Gatorade and a bag of Jalapeño Cheetos and walked around. I looked but never saw my mom. She probably was in an alley looking for dead animals or something. There was a hot woman at the fireworks stand, but she looked like she was working with her husband, who kinda scared me. I sat on a bench to check her out and kept my distance.

They were Native American, and the woman's hair was black, straight, and she wore it down. It had to be at the crack of her ass, and I felt Moby, my friends and I call our junk Moby Dick, get a little hard, imagining what the woman's hair felt like and how she would look naked. *So much for my great night out.* I headed back to the boat; I needed a little privacy. After I did my business, I went back on the deck, and there was another person on board with my parents.

"Markie, this is Ernesto Gombardi. He's going to join us for a day or two," mom said matter-of-factly. This sorry-looking homeless man had like three teeth, was wearing about four layers of clothing and smelled so bad, I almost puked.

"Why don't you introduce yourself?"

I thought my right hand got dirty in the head, but this was more than I was ready for. I smiled and put out my hand.

"Pleasure to meet you, Mr. Gom…" I was so grossed out by him, I forgot his name.

"Gombardi," said my mom.

"…Mr. Gombardi. I'm Marcus Rosewood." It felt like I was shaking the hand of the skeleton Mr. Morris had in anatomy. Poor guy must look anorexic under those clothes.

"Likewise, Marcus. Your mom is such a nice lady. She offered me a ride to Saginaw Bay. You are a lucky young man."

"Yes, I am," I replied, giving my mother a sideways look like she was crazy. Do you live in Saginaw?" I asked to be nice.

"Mr. Gombardi is going to take a shower, and we are going to get him some clean clothes. He's about Father's size, wouldn't you say?" asked my mom.

I'm thinking that my mother's clothes were more his size, but like the good Reverend's son, I nodded my head in agreement.

"I really appreciate this, Mrs. Rosewood. Reverend." He looked at my parents.

"Our home is your home. Even on the water!"

My dad has the habit of saying dorky phrases which annoys the hell out of me. He's always said stuff like 'Our home is your home' for as long as I can remember. He doesn't look the type to be nerdy, so I can't imagine why he does that. We all laughed, and my father went below deck with Mr. Gombardi.

"What the hell, Mom?" I whispered to her the minute I knew I couldn't be heard. "Where did you find this guy?"

"Watch your language, Marcus. He was on the corner, begging for money. It was all I could do to convince him to come on board and have a shower and a meal."

"And you aren't the least bit concerned that he's going to rob us of everything we own, throw us overboard in the middle of the lake, and keep the *Heavenly Lady* for himself?"

"Not in the least. Don't worry, Markie. Your father and I have done this before. We have things covered." "Okay, but that guy is not sleeping with me!"

"I know. He wants to stay on the deck. We've encountered that from homeless folks before. Dad thinks they don't want to impose, but I think they might be a little afraid. You know, the close quarters in the cabin?"

"Whatever," I said. "I'm going to bed. See you in the morning."

"I thought you were a good Christian young man. Go to bed, then, Marcus. Not sure what you're eating for dinner? "

I grabbed two packs of Pop-Tarts from the galley, locked my cabin door, put on my headphones, and don't remember falling asleep. It hadn't crossed my mind that my parents have hosted homeless guests before.

∞∞∞∞

The next morning when I went on deck, there was no one there which was amazing because I never get up before my parents. I looked at the time on my phone; it was 9:17 a.m. *Weird*. I went back to the cabin to use the head and grabbed more Pop-Tarts. I wasn't paying attention and literally ran into my mother.

"Whoa!"

"Sorry, mom. I didn't think you were on board."

"Why wouldn't I be on board?" She was very cranky. She never acted like that at home.

"I guess cuz I never have seen you sleep longer than I have. I was on deck and no one was around. I guess I assumed. My bad."

"Well, we were up pretty late. Your father still is sleeping so keep it down." She paused. "Oh, by the way, how's Mr. Gombardi?"

It was then that I remembered they let that homeless guy shower, eat, and sleep on board last night. "I didn't see him."

69

"That's strange. I'm going to see if he's okay."

"Wait. I'll go with you." We went upstairs, looked on the bow where Mr. Gombardi was supposed to have slept. Didn't see him. Then we went aft. Didn't see him. Even the blankets and pillows were gone. Where was Mr. Gombardi?

June 24 -- Saginaw Bay

No one mentioned the homeless man again. My dad said he probably left in the middle of the night, embarrassed to have accepted our help and food and clothes. After that, it was almost as if he never existed. We docked at Saginaw Bay, the port Mr. Gombardi was supposed to be going. No mention of the man. Oh, we also anchored offshore and used the dinghy. That surprised me because there were plenty of open docks. I just went with the flow; I didn't care all that much anyway.

Saginaw Bay is nice. It was Saturday, and the weekend brought in the tourists. I asked my dad for some money.

"For?" he asked.

"I saw a sign for parasailing and thought I'd try it. What do you think?"

"I think you are braver than I am. Here's $20. Text me when you find out the details. If it's less than $100, and you still want to do it, okay. If not, putt around town. $20 should be enough for food and a movie. Deal?"

"Cool. I'll text you when I have the details. Will you and Mom watch? At least take my picture to prove I did it?"

"Take a selfie. Isn't that what you do now?"

"Dad. I think I'm gonna be holdin' on for my life. Will you take my picture or not?"

"Of course. Text me when you know. I wouldn't miss this for anything."

"Catch ya later."

∞∞∞∞

The beach looked packed, and I noticed a fair share of bikini-wearing blondes. *I'm definitely takin' a stroll on the beach today.* I walked to the parasailing hut. There was a sign that had the different packages:

——

73

Parasail Saginaw Bay

$40 for 500 feet

30 minutes

$60 for 800 feet

Passenger on boat $15

All rides include lesson & photo

All parasailers must sign waiver.

Under 18, parent/guardian signature required.

Sail at your own risk.

I texted my dad, who said they'd meet me at the shack where you registered and paid. I stood in line to sign up.

∞∞∞∞

"Ready to see the view from above?" the 20-something man-bun dude at the counter asked. "The beach has a lot of eye candy today." He laughed.

"I noticed. I want the 500-foot deal. Better view."

"But 800 feet gets them lookin' at you, just so you know."

"500 sounds good. Is there a form for my info.?"

"Are you 18? If not, I'll need a responsible adult signature on this." He handed me a form with room for my information and about 20 or so liabilities they weren't responsible for.

"My parents are walking over. One of them can sign. When do I go?"

"About 45 minutes. Each trip lasts 30 minutes; you're in the air for about 20. Is this your first time?"

"Yeah."

"Nothing to worry about. You're harnessed in and have a life jacket. Even if the line comes off the boat, all you'd do is land in the water."

74

"I'm on a cruiser for two months with my parents. I'm overdue for a little adventure."

"I know what you're sayin'. Let me know when your parent has signed. You can pay then."

"Thanks."

"No problem."

I sat on a nearby bench and filled out my information. I saw my dad walking on the path towards me. "Mom's hunting?" I asked when I didn't see her.

"Of course. Couldn't talk her into it. 'You know how much stuff I find in Saginaw' was her excuse. I think she doesn't want to see you in the air. You are her baby, ya know?" My father laughed and punched my shoulder.

Ouch!! My dad is well-built like I said, and I'm doing okay in the weight room but that hurt. He's 6'1 and I've been taller than him since 9th grade. Helps a lot with basketball. I'd love to play at Michigan State University. I've loved the Spartans forever. The decent thing about Mackinaw Schools is that we have a good basketball team. I was looking forward to my senior year.

"Will you sign this, responsible person?" I asked when I handed the clipboard with the form to him.

"Who, me? I'm not very responsible. At least if I'm not at the church." We both laughed. *Nerd phrase.* Wasn't funny the first time and it still isn't, but I love the guy, so I laugh.

I gave the man-bun guy the form and my dad's credit card. He asked if I wanted my dad on the boat, and I shook my head. I wanted to do this on my own.

"Okay, 'bout ten minutes."

"Thanks, Paul." We fist bumped and I sat down to wait.

"Ten minutes. Want to wait here?"

"Might as well. I'll go back towards the marina when you leave. I saw a good view of someone else on one when I was walking over. Try to wave if you think you can let go for a second." Dad smiled.

"I'm not even that scared. Don't know what'll happen when I start flying though. But definitely don't get me lookin' like a wuss. K?"

"Never. Hey, my rep is on the line, too. Maybe I should go up?"

"Your parishioners will be so disappointed if something happened to you. You need to stay safe."

"Thanks, Markie. That will be my excuse, between you and me?"

I smiled and gave my dad a hug. He really is cool.

"Rosewood! You're up."

"See you from the air," I said.

"Always lookin' up at you, son," Dad said. Another nerd phrase I've heard a million times.

We were on a 19' Searay Sportrider. The instructor gave me a VERY short lesson in parasailing. I had on a lifejacket, and he harnessed the parachute on to me. His partner and he would be holding each end of the sail until the chute was filled with air. Okay, that seems easy. *Shit!*

"Enjoy the ride, Marcus. It's perfect weather for sailing today. When we signal you to come back down, pull this safety pin. Do you want to land in the water or back on deck?"

"Um, water, I guess."

"Cool. We'll circle around and get you. If the sail lands on top of you, don't panic…just swim a few feet. It usually falls behind because of the wind. Ready?"

"I think."

"Chill, dude. You're gonna love this. I can tell by lookin' at you."

"K, let's do it."

While I was in the air, I spent a few minutes practicing how to turn. Then I started looking around. Damn! It was beautiful. The water was incredibly clear. I could see the anchors of the boats in the water.

We were at the end of the beach area, which was pretty wooded and almost deserted. I saw an eagle nest that was bigger than my bedroom on the Lady. Too bad it was empty. The instructor yelled and motioned that we were turning back. I hung on to the steering ropes and tried to stay straight behind the boat. I signaled back with a thumbs-up We turned left toward land, and I started to see more people on the shore.

The south end of the beach was loaded with families. I saw little kids making sandcastles. The next section of the shore had fewer people. Most had on wetsuits…probably snorkeling or diving. When we got to the area with the sunbathers, I saw lots of girls with their bikini tops unhooked, so they didn't get a tan line. I swear I could see their breasts squished into the sand. *Chill, Marcus. Now is not the time to be horny.*

I looked back at the lake for the *Heavenly Lady*. She has a Cherrywood cross on it inlaid into the oak used for the rest of the deck floor. *My Dad!* I remembered to look for him, so I could wave. I saw him waving. I waved back and tried to look cool. I gave a thumbs up while he took some pictures. *Not too hard.*

The guy signaled that it was time to pull the safety pin and float down. I could have stayed in the air all day. I pulled the pin and floated towards the water.

On my way down, I could see the *Heavenly Lady* anchored offshore. It looked like there was something stuck on the anchor. I landed on the water, my sail floated behind me, and I bobbed up and down, screaming like a dumbass. I was so psyched I didn't care. The boat picked me up, and the guys were laughing, knowing they were right. I loved this shit and can't wait to do it again.

June 30 -- Understanding the Story

I never planned to write every day, but to be fucking honest, I am so freaked out about what's going on, I don't know how, or even if I can write it down. Since it's my personal journal, I guess I can say it. I'll definitely be editing before I use this for school. Maybe it'll help me believe this shit is real.

Well, excluding my awesome parasailing experience, the rest of the stop in Saginaw Bay sucked. *My mother is a murderer.* There. It is written. Just like in the Bible. My fuckin' mother befriends homeless people, invites them onboard, then kills them, strips them naked, and ties them to our anchor so their flesh will decompose before the boat gets back to Mackinaw City. Here's the best part: she uses the skeletons for the wind chimes she makes for the bazaar! For the church. I wouldn't have believed it until I saw it for myself.

On Saturday night, Mom brought an old, homeless woman on board. I think her name was Emma. Anyway, it was pretty much the same deal as with the toothless man from Port Sanilac, Mr. Gombardi. When they went down to the cabin (my mom and the lady), I asked my dad what was up with this homeless person stuff.

"It's a way to serve God, of course. You'd do the same, Marcus."

"I hear ya, Dad, but I don't get why she finds the most disgusting person in town. Who knows what diseases they bring with them? Damn, it's disgusting. Sorry."

"Markie, your mom isn't your ordinary Christian. I think you know that. She believes she is doing everyone a favor by using her talents with the guests she brings on board."

"What's that mean?"

"Let's wait for mom. It's time to share a story with you."

"Um…okay. By the way, we need to dive in and check out the anchor before we go. I thought I saw something on it when I was in the air today."

"Really?!"

My dad sounded surprised. He didn't realize the water was clear enough to see 20' down.

∞∞∞∞

About 18 years ago, my parents were on their summer boat trip, and my mom found a dead homeless man while she was digging around in the woods for bazaar stuff. They were in Frankfort when she told my dad that his bones would be perfect for making bazaar items. She knew he'd decompose quickly if he was in the water. My dad wondered if people would know the bones were human. I thought the same thing. She said that a lot of human bones look like other mammal bones, so it would be easy. She told my dad he needed to bless the man to send his soul to Heaven. That night, they went in the woods, got the body, and the rest was pretty much the same.

"I get that, Mom. I can believe you'd do something that creepy for the church. But Mr. Gombardi and that lady were alive. Isn't murder a sin?"

She continued "the story" by sharing how well-liked the wind chimes were and how they hoped they'd find another body for the next year. When they went on the boat the next summer, they didn't find any bodies and people were disappointed at the bazaar. So, my parents decided that putting old, sick, homeless people out of their misery and sending their souls to Heaven was important enough to go through the process of finding the homeless person who looked most in need of their help and suffocating them when they were asleep. I was getting nauseous.

"It's putting someone out of his misery. Mom uses a pillow, and I hold the body because we naturally struggle when we realize we can't breathe. It wakes them up, and when they begin thrashing, I hold them. It sounds terrible, I know, but I pray over them before, during, and after the process. They are out of their misery, son. Can't you see that?"

"Honestly, no, not really. It doesn't sound like a very peaceful death to me."

"Well, it is. Some of them don't even wake up. Marcus; they are living in a body that has passed its ability to survive with any dignity. We are simply letting that soul out of its misery."

"I guess. I mean, it's freaky, but in a way, it makes sense the way you put it. What if they don't believe?"

"They believe. One of the reasons why Mom finds them is because she is so easy to talk with, and she makes certain that they are Christians before she invites them on board."

"Okay, so why am I here? I was hoping you were gonna let me take The Lady out on my own."

"Well," replied my mother, "we were kind of hoping you'd learn the ropes and in a few years, take over for us. We aren't getting any younger."

"You want me to do this? By myself?"

"We thought that James and Trevor might help. The hardest part, by far, is keeping the secret. Even though we know we are serving God, others may not see it that way. We've known the Bonds and the Mandys for years, and you've grown up with the boys. I think they could be trusted."

"Do you?" my father asked.

"Dad…Mom…can I have a few days to think? Ya know, process the whole thing? We're on the water until Friday. How about Thursday night we talk about it? I need some time."

My dad hugged me. "That sounds like a mature idea. Take your time. Ask us any questions and see if you can make peace in your heart about helping these people."

"Okay." The three of us hung onto each other for a while.

I wasn't sure who was comforting whom, but it felt good.

July 2 -- Serving is Not a Crime

Since writing helps me think and remember *(a lesson learned…thanks Mom)*, I decided to write about "the talk" because I needed to let this shit go and begin to absolve myself. I've agreed to carry on the Rosewood tradition. *I feel so fuckin' guilty.*

My parents and I spent more than two hours talking about the Bizarre Bazaar, the name I've given to the entire process of making arts and crafts from human bones. I had a lot of questions. My mother's degrees help her understand how to best take the pain away…that's how she describes suffocating human beings. She knows how to remove the skin and organs without leaving evidence behind. She calls that the remains. Oh, and which bones could be used to make the wind chimes without being detected as human.

The reason they gave me for not hunting animals like bears, deer, and duck was that the hunting seasons were at different times of the year, and neither of them felt very comfortable shooting a gun or a bow to kill for fun. So, I suggested donating the meat to the food bank, and my mother said that hunting just wasn't a proper hobby for a minister.

That makes sense. My ass it makes sense. They still are murderers. "Then how can you justify suffocating a human being!" *I needed a lot of convincing.*

"We aren't suffocating a human, Markie." My mother sat on the bench seat with me and put her hand on my knee. "We are sending a spirit to Heaven. The body has served its purpose on earth. I know you, Markie. You see it too. You need to believe that what you are doing is a service, not a bad thing. I know you understand."

The shitty thing was, I did. Understand. These people…at least the two I've seen so far, had nothing. No family, friends, home, job…nothing. Objectively, it was easy to see as service, to put these people out of their misery, and provide my mother with human bones for church bazaar wind chimes. But shit, I'm the son of an Episcopalian priest, and I was raised with a set of moral obligations I'm supposed to live by. Murder isn't one of them. But service is. A big one. *If I can figure out how to justify this as a good thing, it'll be okay.*

I told my parents I wanted to do it on this trip. I needed to feel it, get through it, and see it as a process…how I think. And I wanted to listen to my mom talk to people, see what she did to convince them and how she knew it was the right one. I love and respect my parents a lot. If I can watch them, do it and still feel the same, I'll know I can see myself taking over. My mom and I would take "the walk" tomorrow in South Haven.

July 3 -- South Haven

Tomorrow is the fourth, and South Haven has one of the best fireworks displays on Lake Michigan. The town was packed with tourists for the celebration. My mom and I left the Lady about 9:00. She was anchored further out than in Saginaw. I asked if she minded if I rowed in, rather than use the motor.

"Yeah, sure, Markie. You okay?"

"I think so. I guess I'm a little nervous. Maybe if you explain what you think will happen, I'll feel better. Make it analytical, you know, a process."

"Okay, Reverend, I hear you." She smiled. "We'll look for items to use for the bazaar. I always have a backpack or a shoulder bag; something for all my treasures. And while I'm digging around, someone usually asks me either what I'm doing or if I needed help finding something."

"Why?"

"Think about it. We're dressed nice and we're digging in trash cans, looking at stuff on the ground, either picking it up and putting it away or holding it for the next trash can. Wouldn't you think it was odd if you saw someone doing that?"

"Hell yeah. Are there people who know you because you've been doing this for so long?"

"Good question. Yeah, sometimes. These shop owners have been here for years. Dad has five different float plans, so we don't hit the same harbor for five years. Still, I've been asked if I'm Debby Rosewood, the lady who makes the stuff for the Mackinaw Bay bazaar."

"What do you say?"

"I don't lie. That wouldn't be right. I talk to them, tell them what I'm doing, and go on my merry way. We hope to release five souls every summer, but when I get noticed, I don't even look for someone to bring aboard. You learn how to be smart about it. Does that make sense?"

"So, having James and Devon on board will mean each of us can do the searching. Then we'd have even more anonymity."

"Maybe. But the one time your dad tried, it was a fiasco. He hated digging in the trash and picking things up, so he looked suspicious. We ended up letting the man he brought back leave in the middle of the night. It changed our timeline."

"How? You can't suffocate someone in the middle of the afternoon."

"Markie! We always wait until it's dark. But we used to bring them onboard earlier, spend time with them, pray with some. Then sometimes they'd make up an excuse to go ashore for a while and never come back. Or they would pretend to be asleep and leave as soon as we went to our cabin. So, we will scout now and if we talk to someone, we'll make plans to meet them later. This first stage is most important; we're looking for a Christian who is in the most need of release. Do you understand what I'm saying?"

"Sure, I know the definition of every word you said. Do I understand it? Not yet. That's why I wanted to come." We were pulling into shore, and I jumped off and pulled the boat to the dock where there were cleats to tie off.

"You don't need to be sarcastic about it," said my mom as she got out of the dinghy herself and huffed as she walked past me to get out of the water. "Well, grab your backpack. We've got hunting to do."

∞∞∞∞

She wasn't kidding. The woman was crazy about what she found, where she looked, and how much shit she put in my backpack or her shoulder bag. It sucked looking in garbage cans and in piles of trash. I did kinda like seeing cool-looking rocks, twigs, dead bugs, leaves, flowers that had fallen off their branch. It felt like we were giving life to an otherwise useless piece of earth. *How ironic.*

We had lunch at an outdoor cafe when my mom stopped listening to whatever I was talking about and was looking around. I was feelin' chill and forgot the real reason we were there. "Hey, earth to Debby. Come in, Mama!" I laughed, but she didn't look at me.

"See that woman over there?" she moved her eyes to the left. Her tone was hushed. I turned towards her line of vision and saw an elderly lady sitting on a bench. It looked like she was talking to someone, but she was alone. She was also dressed in pants, a shirt, a dress, and a coat. It was July 3, and the temperature had to be in the 80's, so I knew mom found someone she wanted to talk to.

"You ready?" she asked. "Let's bring her the rest of my sandwich. They can be suspicious if you just start talking.

Walk next to me and just listen for now. Okay?"

"Yeah. You go. I'll pay for lunch and walk over." I wrapped half of my mom's untouched sandwich in a napkin and picked up her unopened chips as well. *I wanted those for later. Damn!* The waitperson walked over and handed me the lunch tab.

"You look surprised," she smiled. "Were you ready to dine and dash?"

"No…no way uh, Kate. I saw her name on her name tag. I'm with my mom, and she'd probably kick my ass." The waitress was hot, and I knew I sounded like an idiot.

"It's really Katherine, and your mom is like half your size. I'll bet you can take her." She smiled at me again. "Do you need anything else?"

"No thanks, Katherine. I gotta catch up with my mom." I handed her the money for lunch with a decent tip. "No change," I said in my idea of a sexy voice. "And I think you look more like a Katherine. It's a pretty name. I'm Marcus."

She blushed a little and touched my chest. "Thank you, Marcus. Kate's easier for the old people when they ask my name. I like Marcus, not Mark, or Markie."

That brought me back to reality, and I looked at my mom who was standing near the bench but not talking to the lady. "I should go. Pleasure, Katherine." I winked and walked away. *I finally get to flirt and I gotta leave to see if an old lady is worthy of becoming arts and crafts. Fuck!*

My mom was close to the woman but not looking at her. She was listening, and when I got there, I could hear her talking to someone named Robert. She was quiet, but she was acting like someone was with her. "Who do you think Robert is?" I asked my mom.

"Can't tell if it's her husband, a real person or just someone she made up. Let's listen a little longer."

"The tourists think I'm silly to be wearing so much clothing, Robert. You don't think it's silly, do you?" She sat like she was listening to his answer. "Well, if that's how you feel, then go away! Not everyone is as rich and famous as you and has clothes for every season. Good-bye, Mr. Redford. Have a lovely day!"

She was quiet now and was looking the opposite way, watching Robert Redford stroll along the sidewalk.

"Excuse me, Ma'am," I heard my mom say. "Was that Robert Redford who was just sitting here?" She sounded like an excited teenager.

The woman looked at my mom for a few seconds before she felt safe enough to say, "Isn't he gorgeous? We meet on this bench almost every day. I hate when he acts snooty though."

"Oh my, he is handsome. My name is Debby. How do you know Mr. Redford?" She sat on the bench at the opposite end of the woman. "Do you think you could get me his autograph?"

"I can give it to you right now, Debby. Have a bunch of his pictures he signed in my bag. Hold on." She reached into a cart that was packed with shit and handed my mom a black and white photo of Robert Redford from the movie *The Great Gatsby*. In black crayon was his "signature." On the top of the picture was written with the same crayon, **To my sweet Sophie**. Here you go, dear. I'm sorry, but he put my name on all of them. I hope that's okay."

My mom was giggling like a teenager again, holding the photo to her chest, hugging it. "It's perfect. Thank you so much," she looked at the photo to read her name, "Sophie."

Are you sure you can part with this?"

"I got a bunch. It's yours."

"Well, how can I thank you for this wonderful gift? Are you hungry?"

"A little, I guess."

Sophie looked very hungry. *It didn't take me long to get how pathetic these people were. They didn't have anyone or anything. I felt so sorry for her.* "Would you care for the rest of this sandwich, Ma'am?" I asked. Both women looked surprised I was there. *See mom, I have balls.* "My name is Marcus. I'm Debby's son. It's a pleasure to meet you, Miss Sophie." I shook her hand and handed her the sandwich and chips.

"Well, thank you, son. Marcus, you said?" I nodded and sat down next to my mom, forcing her to get closer to Sophie. "You got yourself a looker there, Debby."

My mom laughed, and I acted all embarrassed. "He sure is. And he's a good Christian, too. His father and I are very proud of him. Are you Christian, Sophie?" I was freaked at how easy it was for my mom to talk to her.

"I am. Don't go to church as much as I used to, but I say my prayers every day. Even if He doesn't listen." She took a bite of the sandwich, and I got tears in my eyes. "I've come across some rough times lately, Debby. Sorry. I shouldn't bother you."

"Not at all, Sophie. I've been fortunate in my life and have nothing but respect for those who suffer and keep trying day after day. I don't know how you do it." My mom dabbed her eye with a napkin.

"Well, it ain't easy sometimes," she said as she opened the bag of chips. The sandwich was already gone. I meet nice folks like you, and Robert sneaks a buck or two in my bag every day. It ain't too bad. Lonely though. My husband passed almost ten years ago. There's no one left."

My mom put her hand on Sophie's knee. It *reminded me of last night. I got chills watching her. It scared me for some reason.* "Sophie, dear, I'm so sorry for your loss. May I make a suggestion?"

Mom went on to invite Sophie to the *Heavenly Lady* for a good meal, a shower, and some company. She suggested that they meet at the bench later in the afternoon in case Robert was looking for her. She asked Sophie what she liked to eat and promised her a delicious steak dinner. Sophie hugged both of us when we left, and when I got a whiff of her, the objectivity I needed returned in a flash.

"Oh my God, I can't believe she smell so bad. Do they ever take showers?" I asked my mom as we walked into the grocery store to buy dinner.

"It's the only thing I can't get used to. That's one of the signs I use to be sure it's the right one. Some of them sleep at a church or a shelter, get fed and cleaned up. It's the ones like Sophie who are so lost that they won't take their clothes off because they're afraid they will get stolen. That's why developing trust is so important. And I don't talk down to them. They needed to feel respected."

My mom was putting potatoes, lettuce, meat, bread, and other groceries in the cart as she talked about this like it was a school project. "If I'm at all uncomfortable, I move on. I knew right away Sophie's soul deserves to be released."

We were checking out and as my mom was paying for the food like it was any other day, I decided that we were helping these people. *It's not like the movies when crazy people kill for fun or revenge. Sophie needs our help and spiritual guidance to be where she needs to be.* In Heaven with her husband.

We went back to the boat, and I said I wanted to take a nap. They know I'm not the napping type but didn't say anything. I needed time in my cabin to come to terms with myself. I was already there for my mom and dad. Now I needed to think about releasing Sophie. And now that I know her, she has a name, a face I can recognize, the thought that she would be dead in a few hours made me sad. I lay on my bed and listened to my music. I got myself mentally prepared to do the right thing and let that sweet woman out of that disgusting body she was in.

July 3 (evening) -- The Bizarre Bazaar

We met Sophie at the bench around six p.m. The street was less crowded; it was dinnertime. Sophie apologized that she didn't have time to change. Robert Redford came back to apologize. He asked her to dinner, and she was happy to say that she had other plans. She was ticked off by how rude he was earlier.

My mom held Sophie's basket since she was the only one she really trusted while Dad and I helped her onboard. I asked my mom why we were all going to eat with her, rather than do what we did earlier. "I think she needs the company. Markie, I'm not doing any of this to be mean. I care about every one of these individuals as much as I love you and Dad. It's putting them at peace that gives me comfort; but, it is also showing them that they are deserving, good people. She needs a steak dinner and a little conversation." I agreed.

Dinner was good. Sophie was probably mentally disturbed. She kept seeing Robert Redford watching us as we had dinner. She yelled at him to leave her alone at one point. I hope no one heard her.

After dessert, Mom convinced Sophie to leave her cart and go to the cabin for a shower and some new clothes. It took a while, but when my dad and I said we were going to take a walk on the peer to work off some of our dinner, she agreed.

"Aren't you worried about Mom?" I asked.

"We have signals. She has her phone and can emergency dial if she must. Plus, she can blow the boat horn, flash the lights, or call 9-1-1 if it gets that bad. But I guarantee you, Mom's tough. She can handle herself."

"Is that why you take the men, and she takes the women?"

"Pretty much." My dad seemed like he wanted to be quiet, so I shut up and just walked with him. It felt good by the water. It was a warm day, and the breeze gave me a second wind.

"Well, are you ready to get back? I want to get this moving, so we can finish. I got myself ready, and I don't want to lose my nerve."

"I'm ready. Bless you, Marcus. You are a good person."

95

Sure, hope God thinks so. I got cold suddenly, realizing what the preacher and his family were about to do.

∞∞∞

Mom and Sophie were on the deck when we got back. Sophie was wearing her coat, but she had on a new pair of pants and a flannel shirt. I recognized the shirt; it was an old one of mine, but the pants looked new. I thought about all they were doing for this woman, and I felt peace. Completely. I knew the body who called itself Sophie wasn't good enough for Sophie, the soul inside; it deserved much more. I made a big fuss over how beautiful she looked and gave her a real hug. Poor thing. There isn't any fat to get rid of.

We said we were tired and left my mom and Sophie on deck to make up her bed. When we were in the cabin, my dad put his finger to his lips and got a red pillow out from one of the benches. "It's microfiber," he whispered. "No room for air, so it will happen quicker. Mom will use her hand to make certain it's covering her nose and mouth. Plan on a minute or two. Any questions?"

"How will you know she's released?" I whispered.

"Her eyes will be bloodshot. Happens when no oxygen gets in. I hate that their eyes are open but it's easier to tell. Sometimes we need to check; like when they don't wake up. I don't like to open the lids. It's creepy." My father smiled, knowing damn well this whole thing was creepy. We heard my mom coming down.

"She's asleep. Still has her hand on that cart. She might be a light sleeper."

"Let's give her 15 minutes. Then you can check, and we'll come up on your signal."

The three of us sat at the table and waited quietly. I saw Dad take Mom's hand, and when my mom took mine, I knew they were praying silently. I joined them and asked God for strength and forgiveness. Then I prayed for Sophie…for her to be at peace, to be with her husband, and to no longer need the body she was in. *God, she deserves better. Please gives us the strength to help her.* Amen.

My mom went on deck, and about a minute later, put her foot on the top step to the cabin; our signal that Sophie was in a deep sleep. We walked up the stairs and stood quietly, looking at her. My dad handed mom the pillow, and we walked to her.

I heard my father praying. He nodded to my mom, and she put the pillow over Sophie's sleeping face, pushed hard with her hand over her nose and mouth. My mom had her eyes closed and the creepiest half-smile on her face. She looked like she was…aroused. Sophie jerked and made a few quiet sounds, but in about 90 seconds, there was nothing. She never opened her eyes. Thank God. My mom put her hand out to check them, and I took it and looked at her. "I'll check," I whispered.

She wasn't there anymore. Her eyes were bloodshot and lifeless. I didn't cry because I knew we did the right thing. We left her lying there until about 3 a.m. Being the night before the fireworks, there were a lot of people partying after midnight. My dad came and got me, and we went on deck to get her body ready to put on the anchor. We had to strip her, pull up the anchor with the other two still on it, both almost fully decomposed, and put the body with the others. We splashed a little but we're pretty sure no one heard. My mom cleaned up her stuff by the time we dropped the anchor again. Then we went back to bed and got ready to watch a beach volleyball tournament, a parade, and fireworks.

Today is Independence Day.

July 13 -- Returning Home

The last stop we made was yesterday in St. Joseph, Michigan. Mom and I talked to a few possible receivers, but it didn't "feel" right. I was beginning to understand what she meant by "feeling it." I talked to a man with one leg, who was rolling around on an office chair with wheels. I thought he had to be ready. But when I talked to him, I realized he was an angry old drunk who didn't deserve his peace...yet. We did find a lot of "treasures" in St. Joseph. There were a lot of Fourth of July trinkets lying around. We got a lot of beads and about 100 leis. Mom thought about making wreaths with them.

I was kinda disappointed that we didn't bring anyone on board. I was hoping to do mom's job tonight, which to me, seemed like the most difficult part of the entire process. *Well, there's next summer.* They were hoping that all of us could talk to James and Trevor during our senior year, then the three of us would go out with Mom and Dad as a senior vacation next summer. Then we'd decide if my parents needed to go the following summer, or if we were ready to handle it alone.

July 22 -- One Last Stop

Dad's float plan put us less than a half day trip to Mackinaw City, in the middle of Lake Michigan. He said we wouldn't see boats since we were the middle of nowhere. The last two weeks of the trip involved cleaning bones, getting rid of any items that could be traced back to the three bodies, and organizing the shit we found for Mom to craft.

Cleaning the bones and organizing them was kinda cool. We didn't use the skulls, so I used a sledgehammer to smash them until they looked like sand. Mom used it as stuffing for juggling balls or bean bag sacks. She made sand and bead vases that were used at weddings for a ceremonial blessing. I'm guessing they didn't know the sand was really human skull. My mom taught me a lot about why bones are shaped a certain way, the difference between a male or female, why the teeth last the longest when a body decomposes. Too bad I didn't do this last year when I had anatomy. I would have had an easy A.

I jumped in the water one day, and it was so fucking cold, I made my dad throw me the life preserver.

"You don't need this. Swim back!" shouted my dad as he was laughing.

"See if you can find any cool treasures, Marcus. I always have room for more."

"I cannot believe you guys won't help. I'm throwing both of you in." I climbed the ladder and grabbed them only to let them feel how cold my body was.

"Did you bother to check what depth we're at? Close to 200 feet, according to the depth finder. You know, the instrument on board? I don't know, Deb. Do you think he can do this without killing himself?"

"Devon and Trevor will take care of him, I hope." They laughed some more as my dad gave me a bear hug and mom dried my hair with a towel. *They're crazy.*

∞∞∞∞

I docked the boat in Mackinaw City Harbor at 16:20 on August 10. Dad was impressed. So was I. We had crates loaded and labeled. The ones with the bones said WIND CHIMES.

This is the end of my summer journal. Senior year begins soon, and I'm ready to think about normal stuff. It was a bizarre summer, but I feel like it's the right thing to do…release souls.

October 30 -- Unexpected Truths

Like I said, school keeps me fuckin' busy. Senior year has been a blast! And basketball starts next week. I've been lifting weights three d a week and running three days. Sunday is a day of rest, thank you God!

My mom has been crafting and gave me a wind chime the other day. It was in the shape of an S and made with Sophie's bones. It choked me up; thinking about her again made me wonder if I'll be able to do this. *Why can't we bring them here and have a place they can live?*

I was looking at the wind chime and noticed that one of the phalanges looked different. I thought it looked like a male bone. My mom was making dinner, and I asked her about it.

"They are all Sophie's bones, Marcus. That's what I said."

"Mom, this is not from a female. Look."

She sighed and stopped stirring the sauce she was preparing and took a closer look. She looked at me kinda freaky, then back to the bone. She grabbed the wind chime to look closer.

"Hey! Be careful. I don't want it to break. What do you think?"

"I'm sorry, but I must have made a mistake. There are 48 bones on this wind chime. I don't see why one should matter." She turned away from me and splashed the sauce all over. "Damn it,"

"I got it, Mom. I'm sorry. I didn't think it was that big of a deal. She grabbed the paper towels out of my hand and pushed me away.

"You have no idea what a big deal it is. All these generations, the women in my family have been keeping this tradition alive. And I have one child and it's a boy." She was scrubbing the floor and crying.

"What are you saying, Mom? What tradition? The wind chimes? Releasing souls? I can do it. I know I can." I started crying, too…I don't know why. She was really weirding me out.

"Marcus, there has been a female born to the eldest female child in my family for seven generations. My great-great grandmother was a Chippewa princess. She killed four tribesmen who tried to murder her husband because he was Caucasian. Her tribe used animal bones for making jewelry and small tools and such. My great great grandmother used the bones of the four men to cover up the crime. She taught her children and her children's children how to prep the bones, and that's continued until now. Seven generations, and because of me, it's over."

"I can do it. Why does it have to be a woman?" I was shaking, confused and a little scared.

"Don't worry about it, Markie. I know it will work out. I'm sorry about the bone. I'll fix it."

"Mom, you've taught me the process, you understand the science more than any of your other relatives, so why can't I continue the tradition?" You don't have to change anything on my wind chime. I love it like it is. Don't get upset. It's cool. K?"

She hugged me and said, "KK. Dinner in 12 minutes."

∞∞∞∞

What the fuck! The lady is crazy. My father was in their bathroom, and I pounded on the door. "Dad! I gotta talk to you, now."

He opened the door wearing a towel and looked pissed…Episcopalian priest pissed. "This better be important."

I knew my mom meant 12 minutes until dinner, so I talked fast. My father said he had no idea about the family tradition. "She's proud to be 1/8 Native American, but I never heard about a princess, murder, anything like that. I'll call your grandmother tomorrow. She's the oldest daughter just like your mom. She will know what this is about. Do me a favor, Markie. Don't say anything to anyone yet…especially Mom."

"Why? Do you think it's true? Has Mom ever been mad like that with you?"

"Give me a day to figure this out, Okay?"

"Yeah."

Dad put some sweats on, and we sat down as Mom put the dinner on the table.

∞∞∞∞

It was close to midnight. The house was quiet, and the sound of steady snoring meant it was time.

They'll never understand. I can't break the tradition. At least my sister has a daughter and can keep it alive. I tried to please Mother. I released five times the souls that she did. I thought that hearing the wind chimes would be reminder enough of what the women in this family have done for so long. I found a way to do service AND please our ancestors, but it will never be good enough.

I watched him sleeping for a moment. You are too good of a soul to be me. You are your daddy's son. "Sorry, Marcus. I love you."

I walked down the hall to my bedroom. William, you are an angel. I couldn't tell you what we did. You never would have married me. I never meant to hurt you. I loved you and thought I could be a preacher's wife and a…good daughter of the Chippewa. "I love you, William."

"Dear Lord, absolve me of my sins. Allow me to see my family at peace before my eternal damnation. Amen."

As the door to the bedroom balcony opened, a gust of wind sent the glass doors banging open and closed, enough to break some glass. Debby Ketrick Rosewood let herself fall from the balcony, knowing her future was forever damned.

Epilogue

The Cheboygan Daily Tribune

Murder in Mackinaw City

Mackinaw City Police found the bodies of the Reverend William Alexander Rosewood, 44, and his son, Marcus Allen Rosewood, 17, early Tuesday morning. According to reports, a neighbor heard glass breaking and called 9-1-1 to report a possible break-in. Cause of death appears to be asphyxiation.

Debby Ketrick Rosewood, 42, was found in the backyard of the family home. Her neck and several other bones were broken from an apparent fall from the master bedroom balcony on the second floor. A red microfiber pillow was found by Mrs. Ketrick's body.

Autopsies will be performed to confirm cause of death; however, a spokesperson with the police department told the media they suspect this is a murder-suicide.

The Rosewoods are known for the Annual Mackinaw City Episcopalian Church Memorial Day Bazaar, which kicks off the summer season for Mackinaw City. Mrs. Rosewood was well-known for her bone wind chimes. The family spent two months on Lakes Huron and Michigan every summer visiting ports and collecting items to use for the bazaar.

Debby Ketrick, oldest daughter of…

The End

Book 3

Field of Demons

Dyersville, Iowa

Table of Contents

Chapter 1 -- Baseball and Basilicas

Gary Mooser looked at the itinerary for the upcoming trip to Iowa. "I can't believe I'm going to be in this church," he said to his girlfriend, Danielle Fifner. "I've been studying Basilicas for so long; I can't wait to step inside one. Granted, it's a minor Basilica, but at least it's in the national registry."

"And it's a two-hour drive to Iowa. Visiting basilicas in Italy requires airplane tickets that we can't afford. At least until you get a real job!" laughed Danielle.

"You promised you wouldn't joke, Dani. I know this is way longer than I wanted to spend on my doctorate, but once my dissertation is finished and I have my doctorate, I can teach anywhere. We can go to Italy for sure."

"To visit or to live?"

"Would you seriously consider living in Europe?"

"Yeah, If we're together. I can be a nurse anywhere in the world. I've thought about it."

Gary sat next to Danielle on the sofa and gave her a huge hug. "You are way too good to me, you know that?"

"I do, but I think it'll be worth it." She kissed him, and they made out for a while.

"My shift starts at 7:00, Gary. I gotta go to bed."

"And I promised I'd write 10 more pages tonight. Aaahhh. This better pay off because my manly desires are not being fulfilled, I gotta tell you."

"And that's because…"

"Because you are working overtime so I can spend 100% on my dissertation to earn my doctorate in Philosophy and Religious Studies, get a job at a prestigious college, write several well-renowned books, and enable you to be treated in the manner in which you deserve…like a queen."

I couldn't have said it better myself. Goodnight, my love."

"Good night, Dani."

∞∞∞∞

Gary and Danielle were going to Dyersville, Iowa for five days. Gary wanted to research the church for his dissertation. Dyersville is where the movie *Field of Dreams*, was filmed more than 25 years ago, and the baseball field is still there. The townsfolk dress as the ghost players and play a game every Sunday during baseball season for visitors. Since Gary and Danielle played on a co-ed team and they both love the Milwaukee Brewers, the trip was turning out to be a mini vacation. Gary had to do some work, but Danielle was looking forward to five days off in a row. Dyersville was less than a two-hour drive from Madison, where Gary was a student at the University of Wisconsin.

Gary was almost 30 years old, four years older than Danielle, and had been in college since he was 17. He earned his B.A. and his master's degree in philosophy at the University of Notre Dame. He thought about becoming a Catholic priest, but after he met Danielle, he knew there was no way he could give her up for the Priesthood, not being able to marry and being celibate. He chose to earn a dual doctorate and teach at the university level. They talked about changing religions (they were both born and raised as Roman Catholics), but Gary was deeply spiritual and everything in his heart, mind, and soul told him to teach and not preach.

"Just don't preach when you teach," Dani used to joke around with him about boring professors. She earned her B.S. in Nursing at Notre Dame while Gary was in his master's program. They were both from the Milwaukee area but never knew each other. They were grateful they met when and where they did.

They went to church together every Sunday and chose to live separately. Danielle stayed in the dorms throughout her schooling and spent weekends at Gary's apartment. When they decided that Gary should pursue his doctorate, she moved in with him and began paying all the bills so he could work full time on his degree. None of their conservative parents were very happy with the arrangement, but after a few visits to Milwaukee together, neither the Fifners nor the Moosers could help but give them their blessing. They saw how in love the couple was.

116

The trip to Iowa was the first vacation for either of them since they moved from South Bend to Madison a month after Gary was accepted into the University of Wisconsin's program. The last four years were tough, but neither of them really cared too much for material things; plus, they moved from one college life to another and had no idea what buying a house or making car payments was like. They shared Gary's Toyota, lived in an apartment near campus, and Danielle worked different shifts at the hospital for overtime, so they had no regular schedule. Gary was ready to be done. The trip to see the Basilica wasn't necessary, but he was looking forward to exploring it and being with Danielle. It was more of a thank you to her, a reason to be together for five days, to see the Field of Dreams, the place where Gary planned to ask Dani to marry him.

He'd been thinking about proposing for a while, and when they planned the trip to Dyersville, he knew it would be perfect; their field of dreams was coming true. Everyone but Dani knew he was proposing, an engagement party at Danielle's parent's house was already in the works. Gary's dad offered to let them use his Ford Mustang convertible for the drive. They would drive it to Milwaukee together and be there for the party.

His mother gave him his grandmother's engagement ring for Danielle. She knew money was tight and said he could buy her something new anytime. The ring was platinum, with a half karat round diamond and a leaf filigree design around the ring. Gary's grandmother, Elizabeth Candela, was married to his grandfather Ralph for 68 years, and the ring was willed to their only daughter, Gary's mother, Stephanie. Gary cried when she gave it to him. He said he'd give it back, but Stephanie said it was an heirloom, meant to be passed on, and he should give it to his son or daughter someday.

The plans were in place. A two-hour drive to the Holiday Inn Express, two days of exploration at St. Francis, and a baseball game at the original Field of Dreams. Gary had contacted the owner, Joe Lansin, and shared his plans. He agreed to let them sit on the porch swing so he could propose. One more day of work for Dani; a drive to Milwaukee for Gary to get the Mustang, and they were off. It was going to be a very special trip.

Chapter 2 -- Cruisin' in the Mean Machine

They stopped for croissants and coffee at Humble Bakery near campus. Neither of them wanted to mess up Gary senior's car, so they sat at a table outside the bakery. Neither were big morning people; they were quiet and holding hands on the table. That said more than words for Dani and Gary.

"Do I get to drive the Mean Machine?" That's what Gary's dad called his car.

"Sure. From the church to the hotel. How's that sound?"

"Like walking would be easier." Danielle smiled. "I'd be the one to put a scratch on it. Your father would make me suffer for years if I did."

"He's more protective of the car than my mom," Gary laughed. The caffeine was kicking in and they were beginning to wake up.

"Are you ready for our Iowa vacation, dear?"

"Extremely ready, Mr. Mooser. Wait until you see what I brought for night wear."

"Really?" Money was tight, and negligees and sexy panties weren't in the budget. Dani would fall asleep in her hospital scrubs half the time.

"Yeah, I brought a clean scrub shirt and no pants," she said in her best sexy voice.

"Yeah," responded Gary.

"I'm teasing, fool. I had fun, went a little crazy, and got a few pretty things for myself. Well, actually for you."

"I love you, Dani."

"Oh, you are going to love me even more after this trip, trust me." She gave him a sly, sexy smile and grabbed their trash from breakfast. "Do you want the rest of your coffee, hon?"

"Not in the Mean Machine."

∞∞∞∞∞

The drive to Dyersville was great. They avoided the turnpike and stayed on state highways. It wasn't very crowded, and the drive in the convertible was fun. Danielle's long reddish-brown hair was twisted and in a clip, and Gary, as usual, wore his long, dark brown hair in a ponytail. They made it to the hotel in less than two hours. Gary said the car drove fast all by itself.

Check in wasn't until 4 pm, so they left their bags at the front desk and went to explore.

"Let's walk," suggested Danielle. We've been sitting long enough."

"Yep. And it's still not too muggy. I should walk more at home."

"No, you shouldn't. Finish the damn dissertation. I'm getting tired of double shifts at the hospital."

Gary put his arm around Danielle's shoulder and pulled her close to him. "I couldn't have done this without you, Dani. No. I don't think I would have done this without you. You are my muse." He kissed her.

She laughed. "I'll be your muse tonight, sweetheart. Khaki cargo shorts and a University of Wisconsin t-shirt don't classify as 'muse-wear'."

"You changed my life forever. No matter what happens, you'll forever be my soulmate."

Danielle and Gary didn't talk a lot about their feelings for each other. She stopped walking, turned to Gary and hugged him tightly. "Thank you, Gary. That means a lot. You are my hero; you taught me how to believe in myself, believe in you, believe in life itself. God, I really love you." They stood on the corner of Main Street hugging. They both had tears in their eyes.

"Damn! Where's all this emotion coming from? Neither of us really do this. Do you want me to tell you how I feel more often?"

"No, we're good. I'd have to come up with all these great ways to say I love you. And honestly, Gary, I know you love me, and I know you know I love you; why else would we be in Dyersville, Iowa?" She was smiling.

"The Field of Dreams!" they both said at the same time, laughing as they crossed the street towards the Basilica.

St. Francis Xavier Basilica was the only large building in the quaint town of about 4000. The Midwest is flat, and they could see the towers from their hotel, a little more than a mile away. But seeing it up close was a different site. Its twin towers shimmered in the sunlight, and they both stared at the building.

Danielle and Gary got quiet as they walked through the double wooden doors, dipped their finger in the Holy Water and blessed themselves. Danielle sat in a pew near the back of the church and watched as Gary walked down the long aisle to the altar. *I wish I could take his picture, so he can see how beautiful he looks right now.* There were a few others in the church, sitting by themselves in one of the pews. Danielle felt the same sense of peace as always when in a Catholic church. Danielle was raised Catholic. She attended Parochial schools, and even though she didn't go to church every Sunday until she started dating Gary, she felt the connection inside the walls of the house of God. *Built by man; blessed by God,* remembering what her dad says EVERY time they walk into a church. She understood how he felt.

"Good morning," said a priest dressed in his black shirt and pants with a white clerical collar neatly inserted into his shirt.

"Good morning, Father. How are you?"

"Very well, thank you. I know all my parishioners. Are you visiting?"

"Yes. Actually, my boyfriend, Gary, (she pointed him out to the priest) is a doctoral student at U of W and is here to study the Basilica. His dissertation is about the history of the buildings."

"How interesting. Well, I'll be sure we talk, then. My name is Father Reficul. It's a pleasure to meet you.

I'm Danielle Fifner. Nice to meet you too, Father Reficul."

He walked quietly to Gary, who was now sitting in a pew. The two talked for a few minutes and then shook hands. Father Reficul went to the sacristy and Gary walked back towards her, smiling like a little boy at Toys R Us.

"I'm going to meet with Father Ref. tomorrow. He grew up around here and attended the school and the parish before he left for college. I hit the jackpot."

"Shh," whispered Danielle, as Gary's words were getting louder and louder.

"Sorry. I'm so excited!" They walked out of the church, and he pumped his fists in the air. "This is exactly what I hoped for. Someone who not only is a priest here but also grew up in the parish! It's perfect."

"I've never seen you this excited before. Not about your dissertation, anyway. I think it's kind of cute, actually."

"Shut up. I don't want to be cute."

"Then chill out and feed me. I'm starving!"

One more fist pump and they walked down the block to the diner in town to get some lunch.

Chapter 3 -- A Heavenly Connection

"He is scheduled for 10:00 a.m. mass, then he suggested meeting in the Basilica, so he can point out some interesting details, and we are having lunch after. He asked if you would like to join us. Please do, Dani. You're so good at putting a different perspective on my line of thought; hell, half of my dissertation is from your ideas. Please."

"Of course. Did Father Reficul say where?"

"He said to call him Father Ref. Or Danny. His name is Daniel, but since he grew up here, it's Danny again, like when he was a kid. Oh, and we are having lunch in the rectory with the parish priests."

"How did you get to his first name in five minutes?" Danielle was finishing her Cobb salad, and the waitress brought apple pie a la mode to the table just then. "Thank you, it looks delicious."

Homemade with Dyersville Granny Smiths'. And the ice cream has our own walnuts…tree's out back. Enjoy,"

Danielle looked at Gary and said, "What? We can share. I can't eat this by myself."

"Huh?"

"What?" She took a bite of pie and ice cream, raising her eyebrows expressing her delight. "OMG, have a bite."

"Danielle. We were at the Basilica for two hours. We got to Dyersville at 10:25. It's already 1:30. I talked to Father Ref. for almost an hour." He took a bite of the apple pie and continued staring at Danielle. You okay?"

Danielle looked at the time on her iPhone and said, "Yeah, Maybe I fell asleep. I guess I was so relaxed and at peace, I dozed off. It felt like a few minutes to me. Why are you so freaked out?"

"Don't know. I guess I'm a little pissed at myself for being selfish. I didn't think about how much you need this vacation. I'm sorry Dani. You must be exhausted."

"Not anymore. Especially with this sugar high. You would have woken me up if you heard me snoring, right?"

"With the acoustics in the church, you would have woken yourself up!" Gary laughed and continued to eat the pie. "You aren't pissed?"

"Pissed about what?" She smiled at him.

"What would you like to do next? We could go back to the hotel. Chances are the room will be ready. I could use a nap. Or at least a few hours in bed with my girlfriend in her non-hospital ware."

"Hmmm…sounds intriguing. 'Cept there won't be much sleeping, I hope."

"That's what I hoped you'd say. Let's go."

∞∞∞∞

The hotel room was ready, so Gary took a quick shower while Danielle unpacked and put things away. She smiled when Gary walked out of the bathroom with a towel wrapped around him.

"Good. I'm next. See you in a few minutes. DO NOT fall asleep!"

She kissed him, locked the door to the bathroom and took a fast shower so she could dress in her new lingerie.

"Gary!" she shouted from the crack of the opened bathroom door. "Don't come over here, okay?"

Gary, who is not a snorer, pretended to be sleeping with a loud snort and several wheezes and other annoying sounds. "Promise, Gary!"

"I promise."

She was smiling as she put on the red lace boy short panties and the matching lace tank. She could see her hard nipples through the top and laughed quietly. Danielle was a 32B and her breasts never looked very sexy to her. She was thrilled to see her nipples, hard and erect. *At least he'll get a little something from the girls today.* She turned around to check out her backside, happy that the panties covered just enough to be enticing. Sports and a lot of walking kept her bootie nice and firm. She was petite, so nothing on her body looked voluptuous to her, but Gary loved her ass, and she was thankful it was one of her best features.

"Want some music?" Gary asked.

"Is the pole set up for my show?" she smiled, thinking of herself dancing for Gary. Not a pretty site.

"Oh yeah, it's good to go. I even greased it for you."

"Okay, then let's go Barry White…a slow, sexy one."

"Is there anything not sexy when Barry White sings?"

Danielle walked around the corner. Gary was sitting on the bed, naked, picking out songs to play on his phone. Danielle crossed one foot over the other and put one hand on the dresser. She really did look beautiful. Her hair was down, her lips were glossed, and after about 30 seconds of standing, she made a small "ahem" sound so Gary would look up.

He pressed play on his phone and saw Dani at the same time. He sat on the bed, staring at her. "Wow!" he said quietly. "Wow!" a bit louder. "Damn! You look good!" He got up and stood next to her, rubbing her body with his hands. He wasn't looking at her, and Danielle realized he was watching the two of them in the mirror on the dresser. She used her hands to explore Gary's body, massaging his back and shoulders. They kissed…a long, wet, exploration of each other's mouth. Then Gary picked her up like a bride and lay her on the bed.

"You're always beautiful and sexy to me, Danielle. You," he said, rubbing her front side as he got into bed next to her, "look incredible… beyond amazing." He kissed her, using his fingers to stimulate her nipple.

"They were already hard I was so excited." Danielle let Gary explore her body with his hands and his mouth, bringing her to orgasm more than once. Then, she begged him to be inside her, and with her red lace panties still on, he pulled them to the side and entered her. They became one, and as he began moving faster, Dani squeezed his hard ass cheeks, pushing him deep inside her. Dani had another orgasm and Gary moaned as they came together.

Gary lay in bed afterward, completely happy…and strangely fearful at the same time.

Chapter 4 -- A Haunted Church?

Danielle and Gary walked to St. Francis Xavier's again; the motel was the safest place for the Mean Machine. They left early enough to have coffee, then Gary gave Danielle a kiss and walked to the Basilica. She stayed in the diner and wrote in her journal…typed, really—on her iPhone, expressing her feelings about Gary, about making love with him, in ways that she couldn't or wouldn't verbalize to anyone. She was smiling when the same waitress from yesterday walked over and asked if she needed anything.

"No thank you. I'm just finishing up. I'm sorry I stayed longer than I should."

"Please, honey. It's Dyersville on Friday morning. No one is here until Sunday before the game. Did you know that the townsfolk play a game every Sunday during the season? Been going with my family for years. The kids love it."

"As a matter of fact, that's one reason we're here. My boyfriend is studying the Basilica for his doctoral program, and we are both big baseball fans, so we are taking five days to do them both."

"Awesome," said Millie, the waitress. "I remember you from yesterday; apple pie a la mode."

"That's me. Danielle Fifner. Nice to meet you, Millie." The two shook hands.

"Did you say your husband is at the Basilica? He's not with Father Ref is he?"

"Boyfriend, actually. And yes. Father Reficul introduced himself to us yesterday. He's showing Gary around right now, then we're all having lunch at the rectory."

"Oh," said Millie.

"Why? I would assume everyone around here knows Father Danny. He grew up here, didn't he?"

"Well, technically, yes, Danny Reficul grew up in Dyersville and went to St. Joe's Seminary in Chicago. Had some tough times there; think he even was institutionalized for a while. But he recovered and finished school. Requested to come back to Dyersville. Not the same though; there's something weird goin' on there."

"What do you mean…weird?" Danielle would never have guessed that Father Danny had mental issues. He seemed so kind.

"I've said more than I should already, dear. I'm a Baptist, and we hear all kinds of stories about the goin' ons at St. Francis. You know how small-town folks talk. Only ghosts here are the guys who play in the Sunday baseball games. It's nothing…really."

"Are you saying St. Francis is haunted? That's crazy!"

"Not haunted. Just…oh, forget it. They're just stories. Just stay away from there at night. Okay? They say bad things happen when it's dark."

"Okay." Danielle left a $10 bill on the table. "We'll keep it during the day. Thanks Millie. Have a great day."

"You too, honey. Pleasure chattin'."

Danielle walked across the street to meet Gary and Father Danny. She thought about what Millie said and laughed out loud. *These folks need to get out more often.* Now they think ghosts are everywhere, not just the at the Field of Dreams.

Gary and Father Reficul were sitting on the front steps of the church, laughing about something. Danielle was looking forward to talking with them. And she realized that she missed Gary. She blushed a little thinking about it.

"Hey, you two, what's so funny?" Danielle leaned over and kissed Gary on the cheek. "How was the visit?"

"Incredible. Danny knows so much about the history of Basilicas all over the U.S. Visited a couple in, where'd you say, Father?"

"California and New Mexico. Just beautiful. How are you, Danielle?" Father Ref. shook her hand.

"Great. Thank you. I was talking to Millie at the diner just now. She was telling me about the spooky things the Baptists say about St. Francis." Danielle laughed. "Did you see any ghosts, hon?" she asked Gary.

"Oh, they're only out after midnight. Wouldn't be right interrupting us during mass now, would it?" Father Ref. laughed along with Danielle.

"We did go into the basement, Dani. You wouldn't believe some of the things down there. There were baptism and marriage certificates from the 1800s. It was like going back in time."

"Cool. What did you learn about the church?"

Father Ref. interrupted and said, "Let's walk to the rectory and discuss it over lunch."

"Sounds great. Are we expected? I don't want to intrude on the priest's privacy."

"Not at all, Gary. I told Monsignor Fagan you'd both be having lunch. You'll probably learn even more from the other priests in the parish."

"Sounds great."

∞∞∞∞∞

And it was. There were two other priests in the parish, Father Thomas and Father Ignacio, along with Father Ref. and the Monsignor. The housekeeper/cook, Kantanka served us home-style; we ate turkey chili, cornbread, and Caesar salad. It was delicious.

Danielle helped Kantanka clear the table and serve coffee and dessert (strawberry shortcake) to the priests and Gary. While they were making the desserts, Dani asked Kantanka what part of Russia she was from.

"I grew up in what is now Chechnya. Do you know Russian people?"

"Not a lot, but my best friend in elementary school was Katarina Sokolov. Her parents both were born and raised in Russia and went to college at Marquette. That's where they met, got married and raised their family. Katarina barely had an accent until she was with her parents, who spoke mostly Russian at home. Listening to you reminded me of the Sokolovs."

"Good they got to stay in America, yes."

"I think Mr. Sokolov worked for the government, and I'm pretty sure they became U.S. citizens. Do you have citizenship?"

Kantanka stared at Dani and then smiled. "No citizenship for me. I came here with my husband many years ago. We had two children: daughters.

"Do they still live in Dyersville?"

"Never lived here. We moved to a small town in Ohio. My husband worked for a family from Russia. He did things…bad things for them. I didn't want that life, so I ran away to here. Monsignor Fagan took me in. I was grateful."

"What about your daughters?"

"If I took them, they would have killed me…maybe my Melissa and Katherine too. I had to leave them behind. But I pay the price." Before Dani could ask Kantanka what that meant, the housekeeper took the tray of desserts and went to the dining room. *That was strange.*

Then she sat down and listened as they discussed Gary's doctoral work and what he thought about St. Francis. "Is there anyone around who remembers when the church received its Minor Basilica status. 1956, correct?" asked Gary.

"My parents," responded Father Ref., "were married the year the church was decreed. My father passed nearly a decade ago, but Mother still lives nearby. She is in an assisted living home about five miles outside of Dyersville. She might have somethings to share."

"Only if it is not an intrusion. We don't want to bother her."

"Well, to be honest, she gets angry a lot. She might not want to talk to you about those days. I'm sorry. I bring her communion once a week, and that's about it. She might be uncomfortable talking about St. Francis with a stranger."

"Say no more. I've gotten more than I need and don't want to upset your mother's daily routine."

"Thanks, Gary," said Father Reficul.

Gary and Danielle both got up to go. They shook everyone's hand and thanked them again. Then Kantanka showed them to the door, and a wave of humidity hit them as they left the air-conditioned rectory.

"Did you feel it, too?" Gary asked Danielle as he took her hand and walked across the street with her in tow.

"Hey, slow down! I'm practically running to keep up. And why are we running if you feel the humidity like I do?"

"I'm not talking about the heat. I felt the same way last night in bed. I got chills down my back like something was in the room."

"Come on Gar! Ghosts aren't real. The Field of Dreams was a movie, remember? The townsfolk dress up as dead baseball players. They pretend."

"It's not that. I'm sorry Dani. I know it sounds crazy, but I just got scared all of a sudden. Maybe I felt like the priests know we have sex, and we aren't married."

"Oh my God! We are such sinners. We'll be damned to hell now." Dani was laughing so hard she had to stop and catch her breath.

"Okay, woman. I'm done freaking out. Don't make fun, though. Maybe it was being in that creepy basement. I guess I got spooked."

"Well, I can nurse you back to health if you'd like. I packed some things that may help calm you down. Or at least take your mind off what's bothering you."

"Really? Like what?"

"All in good time Gary. Surprises are my favorite."

"Yeah, when you do the surprising."

"So, I get freaked out when you scare me in the shower! At least I don't think there is a ghost is in there with me."

"Ha ha."

"Seriously, Gary. I know it's hot and all, but you do look a little flushed. Maybe a lukewarm shower together should be first on the list."

"That sounds wonderful, actually. Will you wash my back?"

"And more."

Chapter 5 -- True Love is Forever

Once again, Gary and Danielle spent the afternoon in their motel room, making love and taking a nap.

"I could get real used to this, Gar."

"What? An afternoon nap?"

"Making love AND an afternoon nap. I feel like a rich old lady. But Tuesday'll be here before we know it, and life returns to the same ole same ole."

"Not if you put that on before you get in bed." Danielle wore a sheer ivory Baby doll with matching panties.

Dani laughed. "Right. After I take a shower because I smell like hospital yuck, eat, then find you fast asleep!"

"Well, maybe we need to think ahead…plan a day and night together. I promise you can work a normal schedule after I get a job. Hell, work part-time if you want."

"Ya know, hon, that's not a bad idea. I mean, look at our married friends, especially the ones with kids. They always say they don't have any time for each other. Maybe if we make it a routine…"

"What? Why'd you stop? I love where you're goin' with this."

"What do you mean?"

"When we're married, right?"

Danielle blushed. "Well, yeah, but I didn't want to speak for you. I'm hoping we get married someday. Do you?"

"I guess. I mean, you're a hard worker, your cooking's definitely better than mine, and I guess you're kind of pretty." Gary was tryin' not to laugh.

Danielle looked at him, trying to read his expression.

"You cannot think I'm serious, Dani. Come on!! We're everything but married now. I adore you. You know how I feel. Of course I want to marry YOU. Someday."

"I like that little amen at the end…someday."

"Can you just enjoy the moment and let life happen for the next three days?"

"You're right. What're you in the mood to eat tonight?"

"You know I hate when you ask me that. You plan and right now, I cook. That works for me. Except I'm not cooking anything in this room."

"There's a little Amish town north of here, close to the Minnesota border. I read that they make Homestyle meals on Friday and Saturday and open the lodge to the public. Want to try that tonight?"

"Sounds cool. Should we make reservations? How many do they cook for?"

"Don't know, but the phone number for the only phone in the town is in my contacts. Will you hand me my cell, please? "

Dani called the number and got the last two seats for the 7:00 pm supper, as the gentleman who answered the phone called it. The meal tonight was meat loaf, mashed potatoes and gravy, green beans, homemade bread, and Amish Spice Cake for dessert. "Mooser, for two. Thank you. We'll see you soon. Good-bye."

"See, already acting like we're married," Gary laughed and smacked Dani's butt.

"What?"

"Reservation for two. Mooser is the name. What about Fifner?"

Danielle smiled. "I did just say your name, huh? I didn't think about it. I kinda like it." She leaned over and smacked Gary back."

The couple wrestled and laughed on the huge bed; eventually getting each other excited again. As they were leaving for dinner, Gary and Danielle were both thinking how perfect this vacation was turning out to be.

∞∞∞∞

The drive to Alamakee County was beautiful. Even Gary agreed that Google Maps made finding places so much easier. They kept the top open for the drive and closed it when they got to the lodge because the temperature dropped fast after dark. Especially that far north.

Danielle wore a yellow handkerchief sundress and black wedge sandals. Her hair was down, and she felt like a princess. This was like dressing for the ball since they're usually too busy to go out. Gary wore khaki cargo shorts with a red polo shirt and matching slip-on Converse tennis shoes…no socks. Dani made them take selfies before they left the motel.

The lodge was exactly what they'd imagined it would look like, long wooden tables with benches on both sides. The tables (there we three) were set and had name tags for each reservation. Danielle was happy to see that they were sitting on the same side of the table next to each other. She loved to chat with people, but she was enjoying her time with Gary so much, she didn't want to have to sit across from him.

The room was about three quarters full and there was a trio playing uplifting music as the guests were sitting down. Gary and Danielle introduced themselves to the people sitting around them; mostly couples who lived nearby and told them they were in for a treat. Most of the children seemed to be seated at the far table. *Smart move, folks*, thought Gary.

A bell rang, and Samuel Miller introduced himself and welcomed us to the Alamakee County Amish Lodge. He thanked everyone for being there and recited the menu. Since the 7:00 pm was the last seating, we were welcome to stay after dinner for some light music and good conversation. "Enjoy your meal, friends. Thank you."

The women and young ladies in the community brought out platters of meat loaf, bowls of mashed potatoes, gravy, and green beans. They also set out loaves of warm bread on a cutting board with a knife and fresh churned butter. The bread was in front of Gary, and he cut it and passed it around. There were platters and bowls for about eight people, so Gary and Danielle passed the food around with the couple to their right and the two couples across from them.

141

At first, everyone was fairly to themselves—couple to couple, but as time progressed, they began talking and enjoying warm conversation. Gary and Danielle both shook their heads when Samuel announced the social afterward, but they ended up staying until 11:00 pm, when Samuel again announced to everyone it was time to go.

"That was so much fun," Danielle said when they were in the car. What an unexpected surprise!"

"I agree."

"You were great. Thank you, Gary. I don't know how this vacation could get any better. Well, except for the game on Sunday."

"I almost forgot about that. Are we going to the BBQ before?"

"I'd like to. This vacation is making me feel like we should have our five kids with us," said Danielle.

"Five!"

"JK. Two or three at the most, I think."

"Thank you. But I understand what you're sayin'. Everything is chill and comfortable. I feel very welcomed here. Let's go to the Field of Dreams early and walk around. We'll go to mass at 10:30 and leave from there. Is that okay?"

"Perfect. What are we doing tomorrow? I'm guessing you'll need to work for a while."

"I was hoping to. Maybe you can shop for a few hours. Get some trinkets for the parents. Buy a housewarming present for us."

"Housewarming.? Oh, you mean for when we finally get a house. Okay, that's a good idea. We should do that when we go places. To remind us of the experience."

"I like it. A house, three kids, and the most beautiful wife in town. You'd better give me three hours tomorrow."

"Deal."

Chapter 6 -- Work, Shopping, and the Field of Dreams

Saturday went by too fast for Gary and too slow for Danielle. He was buried deep in his notes and research, and three hours of shopping was more than Danielle could stand. She bought Gary's mom and her mom corncob Christmas ornaments and figured they'd get something at the Field of Dreams for the dads. She didn't want to decide on the first "housewarming" item herself, so she'd text Gary pictures of things she saw. He eventually asked her to decide and let him work. She felt bad long enough to remember she wanted the shit done even more than he did. She ended up with a handmade stained-glass window plaque of St. Francis Xavier Basilica. It was small but all she could afford. It would look beautiful hanging in a window and was a great memento of the trip.

Dani brought Gary McDonalds and showed him what she bought while he took a quick break and ate. He loved the stained glass and kissed Danielle for choosing the memento. "The Basilica is about me, though," he said.

"You are about me," said Danielle. "So, it works." She paused, "Ya know, we've been extra lovey-dovey these past few days. Think there's something in the air? Maybe that's where your scary feelings are coming from. Do you think you can live with the same person for the rest of your life?" Dani acted scared and fell back on the bed.

"Woman!" he responded. "I'd have been gone a long time ago. I know what a great thing I've got and am not planning on going anywhere without you. Got it?" Gary fell on the bed next to her and began tickling her. He knew she hated it, especially on her feet.

"Stop! Okay, I got it. Get back to work."

"What're you gonna do if I don't?"

"How 'bout find a man with a job! I'm going to go sit in the lobby and read so you can work. How's it going?"

"Very well. I'm incorporating my notes into what's already written. It didn't feel right to keep it separate. The work is about Basilicas, not St. Francis."

"Good point. That makes it harder, though. Huh?"

"Of course, but it's worth it. I think I'll be ready for you to do a full read by next weekend." Danielle read a section at a time to edit any typos or grammatical errors. Gary asked her to read the completed dissertation before he submitted it for review at UW.

"Wow, really? I didn't realize you were that close."

"We are that close. And thank God, because it's been way too long."

"But it's almost over. And then we get to live: a mortgage, car payments, diapers for Gary Jr." Dani was laughing.

"I know you are being facetious but that sounds pretty damn normal and really, really good."

"It does."

∞∞∞∞

Gary and Danielle woke up to 20-degree cooler temperatures and lower humidity. Midwesterners expected the hot, humid summer weather and dealt with it, and days like this were a treat.

Gary wore slacks to church and brought his khaki shorts for the ball-field. Danielle wore the sundress that she wore to dinner on Friday, adding a white shrug to keep her warm. She was going to change too; she played short stop for the co-ed team and didn't get pushed around by the guys. The field of dreams had bats and gloves and balls for visitors to play with, and she wanted to hit a ball into the cornfield. And she could, if she got the right pitch.

Monsignor Fagan said the mass, and Gary and Danielle held hands during the sermon which was regarding love and commitment. The second reading was Corinthians Chapter 13 about faith, hope, and love. "And the greatest of these is love."

After church, Gary and Danielle went to the diner for a light lunch and changed in the restrooms. As they were eating, Danielle smiled and commented, "I have loved every moment of this adventure, Gar. Not being at the hospital has been a treat, being together is a gift, and if I keep eating this much, I might weigh too much for the Mean Machine."

"Stop! So we indulged for a few days. I think Dad's car can handle a few extra pounds. And I'm talkin' about both of us, so don't get sensitive." Gary laughed because Dani is not the "sensitive" type. "Are you ready?"

"Let's do this!"

It was about four and a half miles from town, opposite of their motel. Danielle bought a few granola bars, two bottles of water, and some bubble gum at the register before they left the diner. "Ya never know if we'll need food and water."

"What's the gum for?"

"Oh, I plan on puttin' one in the cornfield today. You know I have to blow bubbles when I bat!" They laughed as they sat in the car while the roof went down.

Gary was nervous. This was proposal day. He called Joe Lansin yesterday while Danielle was shopping to be sure he remembered they were coming. His grandmother's ring was in the pocket of his shorts. He was worried all during church that it would be gone when they got back to the car. *It's Dyersville, Iowa.* He also thought that he probably got spooked those two times because of the marriage proposal. The long weekend was perfect; he was certain Danielle was going to say yes. *What do I have to worry about?* He smiled.

"What's the smile for?" He and Danielle had been quiet on the short drive to the Field of Dreams. "You look like you have a secret." She put her hand on his over the drive shaft.

"No secrets. Just happy. And excited. Look."

They could see the baseball field as they were driving on the long winding road that was exactly like it was in the movie. Gary stopped, and they looked at it for a moment.

"I am so excited!!" shouted Danielle as she kicked her feet and did her own fist pump.

Gary laughed.

Chapter 7 -- The Proposal of Their Dreams

There were a few families there, and Dani got her turn to bat quickly. One of the guests pitched to her and asked Danielle if she wanted it underhand.

"Only if it's a softball. If so, fast pitch, please."

The man gave her an "okay, I'll pitch it normal." She got in her batting stance and waited for the pitch. She swung and hit it, foul, into the first base outfield.

"Ready for another one?"

Danielle blew a bubble and nodded her head. *Oh God*, thought Gary.

This one was perfect; dead centerfield, lost in the corn. "Did you see that!" Daniele was screaming and jumping up and down as she ran the bases. The other visitors were clapping for her. Gary was at home plate waiting for her, and she jumped in his arms and they twirled around.

"Nice swing," said an elderly gentleman as he walked over to the happy couple. "I'm Joe Lansin. Welcome to the field of dreams." They shook hands with the owner, and Joe winked at Gary as he walked away to meet the others. That was the signal that everyone was out of the house, and Gary and Danielle could share their moment privately.

"Want to take a walk?" Gary asked as he put his hand on his shorts to check for the ring for the tenth time.

"Sure."

Gary took Danielle's hand as they walked along the path to the house. Danielle was talking about her home run, but Gary was only half listening. His mouth was getting dry, and he wished he'd brought the water they had in the car.

"Are we allowed to be here?" she asked as they stepped on to the front porch. Look, there's lemonade and two glasses. Maybe we should stick to the path."

"Okay. But it's the same porch swing from the movie. Can't we just sit for a minute? If someone says something, I'll apologize, I promise."

Danielle looked at him and smiled. "That's what I was hoping you'd say!" She ran to the porch swing and patted the seat for Gary to join her. As soon as he sat down, she crossed her legs up under her and looked out at the baseball field. "Do I look like Annie?" Annie was the name of Kevin Costner's wife in the movie.

"Much better," responded Gary. He stared at her.

"What?" she asked.

Well, now is as good a time as any, thought Gary as he stood up and knelt on one knee in front of her. "Danielle Anne Fifner, you are the love of my life. I want to be with you forever. Will you do me the honor of being my wife?" He reached in his pocket and held the ring between his thumb and finger for her to see.

Danielle knew it was coming, someday, but was in shock that this was happening on the porch swing of the Field of Dream's house. She smiled and nodded yes as tears began falling from her eyes.

"Will you say it, so I know it's really real?" Gary was smiling and crying too. It was so weird for either of them to be emotional in public, and here they were, in front of a bunch of strangers and they were both crying and smiling.

"Yes. Yes, I will marry you. Yes, I will be your wife. I cannot believe you made this happen, right?"

Gary didn't answer. Instead, he put the ring on her finger, leaned in and kissed her warmly. "The lemonade is for us. Mr. Lansin is going to take our picture. And yes, we've talked before today."

"I can't believe you planned this! It's perfect, Gary. Thank you. The ring is beautiful. It looks antique." She was admiring the ring as Gary stood up and poured them lemonade.

"It was my grandmother's. She gave it to my mom, and my mom wants us to pass it on to one of our children."

"How special. I love it. And I love you, too."

"She said YES," Gary shouted as he raised his glass of lemonade. A group of several dozen people began to clap and cheer. Mr. Lansin was standing close to the front porch, waiting to take the picture.

"Have they been there all along?" asked Danielle, somewhat surprised.

"No. We had privacy for the proposal part. The signal for the picture was when I poured the lemonade. Joe must've brought the people along."

"It's perfect."

"Yes. Our field of dreams. Our future begins here." Gary put his arm around Danielle's shoulder, and she put her head on his. Mr. Lansin took several photos with his cell phone which were being automatically uploaded to Gary's.

After the photos, Danielle and Gary joined the group for the pre-game BBQ, met some wonderful people, played catch in the yard together, then finally sat on the bleachers for the game. Someone had a speaker and microphone and was the "announcer." As the players' names were called (Shoeless Joe Jackson, Moonlight Graham, Buck Weaver, Eddie Cicotte, etc.) the crowd cheered.

The game was a blast. They sang the national anthem, had a 3rd inning stretch (because there were only four innings), did "the wave", cheered for the players, and laughed when the umpire threw one of the players out of the game for arguing. All in all, it was perfect. The "ghosts" were very entertaining. Danielle thought they were good enough to have been in the movie themselves.

Chapter 8 -- Father Ref. to the Rescue

The newly engaged couple walked back to their car hand in hand. Even though it was just getting dark, the lights for the stadium were on for effect. Gary and Danielle stopped to take a few more pictures and got in the car.

"I hope our dads like their Field of Dreams baseball caps," said Danielle.

"I'm sure they will. Let's go so we can get to the main road before dark."

"Do you want me to Google Map the return route?"

"No. I think I've got it. What a fun day. Did you enjoy it?"

"Not really. I had to get engaged! It kinda put a damper on things. And look at this ring my fiancé gave me. Can you believe he planned the whole thing behind my back? Even had lemonade to drink like in the movie." Danielle leaned over and kissed Gary. "This has been the best day of my life, Mr. Mooser."

"Fiancé. That sounds real good."

"I agree. And I like Mrs. Mooser even more. And I'm not talkin' about your mother, ya know?"

"Well, Mrs. Mooser-to-be, I can't wait to call you that." The Mean Machine suddenly swerved on the road, Gary immediately focused as it turned around and stopped quickly in a ditch. The car was sitting on its back tires and Danielle and Gary were both in shock.

"Are you okay?" they both said to each other at the same time.

"I'm fine," answered Danielle. "What happened?"

"Me too. I think I hit something. Or blew a tire. I don't know. Let me get out and you crawl over to the driver's side, and I'll help you out."

Gary and Danielle got out of the car and walked back to the road. They couldn't see anything wrong with the car, other than that it was in a ditch. It was almost dark, and when Gary tried his cellphone, he had no battery power left.

"I told you to charge it," laughed Danielle as she got out her phone. "No service. Damn. We need to get back to town. How about I used the flashlight on my cellphone which still has a 72% charge by the way, and you carry me on your back since I wasn't planning on walking back to the motel tonight."

"Seriously? It's like three miles to town and another mile to Holiday Inn!"

"I'm kidding. But you owe me."

"Fair enough. Let's go."

The couple began walking on the dark, deserted road. "I can't believe not one person drove this way from the field," said Dani as she rubbed her arms trying to keep warm. The night air and all the large trees kept the temperature cooler than usual.

"That does seem kinda strange. We did stay and take the pictures. Maybe we were the last car to go this way. Still, you'd think one car would drive by." Gary put his arm around Dani to keep her a little warmer.

The two walked in silence for a minute and as they walked around a curve in the road, saw a car coming towards them. "Yeah!" said Danielle. "Do you think they'll stop?"

"It's Iowa, hon. Everyone stops."

"You're so weird," she joked as she saw the car even closer and began waving her cellphone back and forth, so the driver could see them. The car did slow down, and when the driver window came down, Gary, Danielle, and Father Reficul all laughed. "Thank God!" said Dani.

"Father Ref., what are you doing out this way?" asked Gary. "Our car is in a ditch about a mile back. We're so glad to see you."

"Thank God is so true," responded Father Reficul. Hop in. Let's get back to town so we get someone to pull your car out of there."

Gary held the door for Dani, then walked around the car and sat in the seat next to Father Ref. He asked, "What brings you out this way?"

"I was with my mom this afternoon, and another one of the residents at the retirement home is the father of a couple who lives out this way. Judy and Phillip Page. Phil's dad turned 100 years old this winter. He's still got a lot of zip in his step. I always enjoy talking with him when I go see my mom, so I'll ask the Page's if they'd like to drive out with me. The two of them are in their 70s, so it works well for everyone."

"How nice," said Dani. "How was your mom today, Father?"

"Call me Danny, Dani." Father Reficul laughed at his words. "I've wanted to say that since the day I first met you. Sorry to laugh. Father is fine if it's best for you."

"So, Danny," said Dani, "how's your mom?"

His voice hardened a bit. "Well, fine. If you're almost 40 and want to be treated like you're 13."

"What's that mean?" asked Gary.

"Oh nothing. My mom likes to tell everyone what to do. Always has, always will. It pains me to visit her and feel so let down after I leave. Brings out the guilt. You know what I mean?"

"Oh yeah. It took both of our moms and dads a few years to get used to us living together even though we were adults. Kinda gets old, huh?"

"Gary! Maybe Father Ref. doesn't approve either."

"No worries, Dani. I'm not your conscience. You're old enough to make your own decisions."

"Thank you. And now that we are engaged, it's almost like being married." Dani said, a little embarrassed talking to a priest about living together. *God, Catholic guilt never goes away.*

"Engaged? When did that happen? Congratulations." Father Danny held out his fist for Gary. "Way to go."

"This afternoon on the porch swing at the house at the Field of Dreams. It was perfect. Gary planned the whole thing without me knowing."

"That was sneaky, Gary. I'm impressed," said Father Ref. "I have a hard time keeping secrets. How'd you do it?"

Gary smiled. "I don't know. I wanted to make the proposal special, so when this trip came up, it all kinda fell into place."

"Well, congratulations. You two make a great couple. I think I knew you were meant to be the first time I met you at St. Francis. What a perfect ending."

They stopped in front of the Basilica and Father Reficul shut off the car. "Let's go this way. I need to get something from the sacristy. Then we'll see who we can call to get you out of that ditch."

"Father, I'll call AAA. And I can use my cellphone. Okay, Danielle's cellphone."

They were walking up the steps of the church as Father Reficul was unlocking the door. "Let's go," he said as he opened the door and walked in the church, not waiting for Gary or Danielle.

"That was strange," Dani quietly said to Gary as they opened the door. "He's in a hurry."

"I guess. We really don't know him that well, do we? Maybe's he gets grumpy at night."

"Or maybe he's still pissed off at his mom," replied Dani as she automatically dipped her finger in the holy water and blessed herself.

"We're in a church, Dani!"

"Oops! My bad. Sorry, Daddy."

"Ya know, fiancé, you sounded like an ass cussing in a church...a Basilica at that!" Gary laughed at teasing her because Dani looked like it bothered her. "I think God's cool with us, hon."

"You're right. Catholic guilt. I feel like my parents are here." She laughed with Gary. By now they were near the altar of the church, and they could hear voices, Father Reficul for sure, but several others as well in the sacristy. They looked at each other and recognized the distress on their faces. A gust of cold wind somehow came from the back of the church, blowing out the candles on the altar and leaving Gary and Danielle in darkness. A chill ran down their spines.

Chapter 9 -- The Ghosts of St. Peter's

"Where the hell did that come from?" Gary said. "The doors are closed."

Danielle moved closer to Gary as the two of them heard laughter in the sacristy. She looked at Gary, clearly afraid. "Gary!"

Gary whispered, "It's okay, Dani. We're tired, and I know I'm thinkin' about what the waitress said to you. But at the same time, I'm smart enough to know nothing bad's gonna happen. This building is old; I'm sure there are drafts. Why don't you call AAA and maybe we can sneak out of here?"

"Good idea." Dani took her phone out of her pocket and looked at it. "No service," she frowned. "I had service the other day in here. Why not now?" She sounded concerned.

"Who knows. Maybe they shut the cell tower down at night. It's Dyersville, Iowa, Dani. Some of these people don't have cell phones, ya know."

"You're right. Father Reficul!" she shouted. "Can we turn some lights on? The candles blew out on the altar. It's pretty dark in here!"

Gary was impressed with her assertiveness. He suddenly felt more relaxed and was laughing at himself.

No one answered.

"Danny!" This time it was Gary. Maybe he hadn't heard. "We're in the dark in here. Could you please put some lights on?"

They waited. Again, no answer. They heard a hissing noise on the altar. Dani thought of a snake, but a huge flame from an invisible structure immediately lit up the altar. Then, organ music began playing a somber, unearthly song. It reminded Gary of a funeral march. He pulled Danielle closer to him. They didn't move.

"Welcome to the Black Mass, my pristine, ignorant young friends." Someone walked from the sacristy to the front of the altar. He was wearing a long, black hooded robe that looked nothing like a priest's vestments. The hood covered the man's face. "I'm so pleased you were too naïve to figure any of this out." The man took off the hood, and Father Reficul, looking nothing like the warm-hearted, kind priest they'd met just a few days before, revealed himself and smiled. His gums and lips were bright red, and his white teeth were glowing. "Please, join us."

Three other hooded people walked from the sacristy to stand beside Father Reficul. Gary and Danielle, who still were not moving, were terrified; *Is what Millie said true? Are we dreaming? Is that really Father Danny?*

Father again asked the two to join them, and when neither moved, shouted, "Ascend the altar of Lucifer! Now!"

They were numb with fear as they slowly walked up the steps to stand face to face with the demon who called himself Father Danny Reficul.

"Very good, my children. Please meet my friends. To my far right is David Koresh, former leader of the Branch Davidians. The man removed his hood to reveal a hideous-looking man with scars all over his body—like from a fire. Once the two looked past the scars, they realized it was Father Thomas.

"And to my near right is the Reverend Jim Jones." The next thing to remove his hood was Father Ignacio, now looking more like a corpse with a greenish face, sunken eyes, and a hole in his head. "Yes. This is the great Jim Jones who will always been known for the Revolutionary Suicide of The People's Church."

Danielle sat down on the step of the altar. Gary joined her to be sure she was okay. Her skin was white, and she was shaking. Gary was doing his best to be there for her, and his own fear was obvious.

"And of course, our Monsignor Fagan." Father Reficul shifted his head to his left. The most deserving always sits at the left hand of the Master. I give you Judas Iscariot!" Father Reficul laughed as Monsignor Fagan removed his hood to show his face. He looked the same, except evilness exuded from his body; and the noose and the marks around his neck weren't there when the group on the altar had their family-style lunch together the other day.

"What are you doing, Danny?" asked Gary, voice firm, not showing his fear. "Is this your idea of a sick joke?"

"Silence! The scum will not speak. Do you not understand where you are? This is no joke. This is my home. I am Master of All. Some call me Satan, some Beelzebub, others Lucifer. When my parents, the scum who married my Angel, came to this small town, they opted for Reficul instead of Lucifer. The male scum could not bear to reveal our greatness.

"But when I learned who I was while in seminary, I commended myself to the life of Lucifer. And to honor Mother, an Angel of the Original Himself, I killed my scum father without hesitation."

He paused, looking at Danielle, who thought she saw compassion in his eyes. "Why are you looking at me?" she asked.

"Because Mother Angel has requested a sacrifice. And you, Miss Fifner, are it. Mr. Mooser," he looked at Gary, "I shall permit the return your grandmother's ring. I believe in the love of family?"

Danielle and Gary looked at each other, confused by what Lucifer was saying. Then Mr. Koresh and Reverend Jones grabbed Danielle and brought her to the Holy Table on the altar. When Gary tried to run to her, Monsignor easily stopped him, using his noose to tie him to a chair used by the altar boys.

Danielle was screaming and struggling to get away, but the men overpowered her. The Holy Table was covered with a black cloth, and the men were using silver chains to stop Dani from moving. They wrapped them around her as they chanted in a language neither Danielle nor Gary understood. The design of the chains looked like an upside-down crucifix, and when Reverend Jones took off her shoes and tied her feet together, she screamed again.

"May our Father receive this sacrifice before us with glory and honor. Stop the beast from that wretched screaming!" he shouted.

Gary saw Kantanka, the housekeeper at the rectory, bring a roll of duct tape to David. She walked with her eyes down, not looking at anyone, especially Danielle. Gary, who was also screaming for them to stop, was silenced by a few strips of duct tape too. After a moment, he gave up the struggle and began to cry.

Danielle was still as she watched Lucifer walk between the other two demons and lifted his arms. "By the grace of the Original, for Mother Angel, for the first betrayer Judas, for hatred and abomination to remain on Earth forever, we commend your soul to hell. He picked up a large, shiny knife with a black engraved handle and lifted it in the air.

Danielle turned her head and met Gary's eyes. She looked at him with nothing but love, and Gary returned his love with tenderness. Neither of them was ever much for words, and when the blade entered her heart repeatedly as Lucifer and the others chanted their unholy melody, Gary knew his bride-to-be was on her way to Heaven. A soul as loving as hers would send Satan himself running if she went to hell. That's what he kept telling himself again, and again, and again.

Epilogue -- Ten years later

Professor Gary Mooser, dean of Philosophy at the University of Chicago, was one of the favorite professors on campus. He was open and honest with his students, didn't hold back his beliefs and practices, and answered the same questions about the night in Dyersville every new semester. He said it was good therapy for him to relive that night in a classroom environment. He said it made the event less personal. He never talked about his stay at Chicago Lakeshore Hospital, where he became indoctrinated to the ways of St. Francis and its unholy inhabitants. Nor did he reveal his second-self, Stephen Paddock, Las Vegas shooter responsible for almost 60 deaths.

"So, the test tomorrow will cover Native American, Puritan, and African American philosophies that have influenced the United States. Expect to do some writing that gives your opinion and uses our discussions and references from the class to argue your reasoning. Any questions?"

"Dr. Mooser, do you think Reverend Jones studied W.E.B. DuBois and Alain Locke?" Both were African American writers and philosophers who wanted to bring an end to the perception of black inferiority to both whites and blacks. "I mean, there were a lot of African Americans at Johnstown, right?"

"Ms. Constantini, I have not studied Jim Jones' history, and I really don't care what he thought. "Yes, almost a third of the victims in Johnstown were African Americans, but why he lured the people he did to follow him has less to do with his studies, and everything to do with his charisma, his good-looks, and his keen sense of people. He could manipulate on his own; if he ever read DuBois or Locke is irrelevant, really."

"Yes. Thanks, Doctor Mooser."

As the class walked out of the room, Dr. Mooser followed behind to his office on the first floor of the philosophy and religious studies building. The Dean's office had a window looking out over a courtyard. It was November, and snow was already on the ground; but today the sun was shining brightly. Gary could see the reflection of the Basilica of St. Francis Xavier through the shade on his window.

He opened the middle drawer of his desk and picked up an antique engagement ring and gently rubbed the diamond with his finger. *I know now we could never have been together, Danielle. You wouldn't understand this power.* He put the ring back in the drawer and turned his chair around to look at the stained-glass basilica. *See you this weekend, Danny.* He smiled as a large cloud covered the sun and turned the world gray and cold.

The End

Book Four

Precarious Polly

Udall, Kansas

Table of Contents

Prologue -- May 25, 1955

Despite the tornado warnings, Richard Magnum was in his barn, securing what he could…just in case. When he heard the cracking of tree trunks, he knew it was close. The wind refused to let him open the door.

"I'm sorry Linda!" he screamed as he opened the storm cellar door and went down the steps. *She'll go to the basement.* He sat on the dirt floor, sobbing as he heard the sound of a train racing through his backyard knowing his wife never woke up.

∞∞∞∞

On the other side of town, Joseph and Ethel Oren woke when they heard the wind. "Polly!" shouted Ethel as she ran to her 5-year-old daughter's room, her husband at her side. Mrs. Oren grabbed her sleeping daughter as the tornado lifted the roof like a band aid being ripped from a child's skin. When a heavy metal floor lamp struck and killed Joseph and Ethel instantly, Polly flew out the open roof, leaving her parents strewn on her bedroom floor as the red ribbon holding her hair floated near her mother's lifeless hand.

Part One

Family Reunion

Chapter 1 -- The Tale is Told

Most Midwestern towns are quiet places, where teenagers stealing bikes, bar fights between best friends, or the occasional natural disaster, are the stories that make headlines in the local paper. Life in the small Southeastern town of Udall, Kansas was exactly that. Udall's claim to fame is the tornado on May 25, 1955, which killed 80 of the town's 610 residents, injured more than 100, and with the exception of one house, destroyed the town. Everyone was affected by the storm, and now, generations later, a stone monument memorializes those who died. It took a while, but the town was rebuilt, and the spirit and soul of Udall were restored.

One of the names on the monument, Polly Oren, was a little girl whose body was never found. Her parents, Joseph and Ethel, were beneath the rubble on the second floor of their home. The storm blew the roof off. They were in Polly's room, her mom's hand outstretched as if it were reaching for a red ribbon that everyone knew was Polly's.

A story was born about the child. Precarious Polly wreaked havoc on the small town and left future residents in pain and sorrow. There were many skeptics, and I, Rick (Richard III) Magnum, was one of them.

∞∞∞∞∞

My grandad married my grandma Rachel six years after he lost his first wife in the tornado. They had five children; my dad is the youngest. The second week in August is the annual Magnum family reunion. The traditions remain the same. We have the Magnum Olympics, a Thursday evening BBQ, a volleyball tournament, and the story. My dad, Richard II, sits against a bale of hay in the barn surrounded by four generations of Magnums and tells us about Precarious Polly.

Chapter 2 -- The Story Must Be Shared

We've all heard about the tragedy that struck Udall on May 25, 1955. The F5 tornado that night destroyed the entire town, killed 80 people, and took one little girl's body somewhere between this world and the next. Polly Oren, a precocious, bubbly Kindergartener with long, brown braids, was fast asleep in her tiny bedroom, decorated like a cottage. The seven dwarfs were painted on her wall and a tea set sat on the round table in the corner, near her stuffed animals and her beautiful Snow White doll.

Polly's mom, just as she did every night, tied Polly's braids with a long red ribbon, weaving them together so her hair wouldn't get tousled through the night. After her prayers, Polly's mom read a story. Oddly, that night's tale was The Wonderful World of Oz about Dorothy Gale, who goes to a magical land after she is taken by a powerful tornado that struck her small Kansas town. The book, along with Polly's red ribbon, were on the floor next to the bodies of her mother and father. Polly was nowhere to be found.

This is the point where Dad would pause, and the flame of the lantern would flicker (probably the breath of one of my uncles). It gave me goosebumps the first time I saw it.

They said that Polly was taken by the winds of the tornado, and the force of the vortex undid her braids, tangling and disheveling her beautiful hair. Her Snow-White nightgown was ripped and muddied as the debris in the funnel cloud zoomed past her. When she finally landed, she was no longer pretty Polly Oren. Alone in a large field of corn, scared and cold, she wandered until she fell asleep from exhaustion.

How she survived, no one knows. (Another pause.) *When she visits Udall, she leaves a red ribbon behind. Remember, Precarious Polly isn't the sweet little girl who was taken all those years ago. She is. . . I don't know. . . an aberration that every time it returns to Udall, someone dies. Not every tornado brings a visit. And it's not always a storm when she leaves her message behind. Most of the ribbons are dirty and worn; looking as though they fell from inside a tornado. They all have brought pain and suffering to the loved ones left behind.*

Before you leave this barn, remember: if you ever see a red ribbon lying on the ground in Udall, DO NOT TOUCH IT! Please keep our family safe from the misery brought by Precarious Polly. Please!

He is a great storyteller and scares the kids every year. Eventually, he and the other adults laugh a little and remind us that ghosts aren't real, and Polly makes a great story.

That is... until the summer of '04 when my cousin Fred found a dirty red ribbon on a bale of hay.

Chapter 3 -- What Was That?

I was 15 years old when Fred saw the ribbon. "Did you put this here, asshole!" he shouted at me. The two of us went to the barn alone early in the morning to see what we could do to scare the younger cousins during the story.

"Fuck! No way, Fred. Maybe my dad wants to scare us all tonight. I'll bet he put it here." The two of us stared at the dirty long red ribbon like it was pornography…something forbidden yet seductive. Fred had jumped on the bale of hay for fun and it kinda just slipped off the top. It landed on the floor, clearly visible.

"Do you think it touched me? Not that I believe in Precarious Polly, but your dad sounds pretty adamant about not touching the ribbon."

"I don't think so. I didn't even see it until you stood up and it was on the floor. Naw. You didn't touch it."

"But do you think it touched me?"

"What? What's the difference?"

"What if I jumped on the hay and it was there, and I hit it without knowing I did? Ya know, accidentally? Is that the same as if I picked it up? I mean, do you think the curse applies if I touched it accidentally?" Fred and I were still staring at it.

"There is no curse, asswipe! It's a scary story people in this little town made up. Come on, Fred!"

I didn't want to tell Fred that I didn't think it mattered whether he purposely touched the ribbon or not, but I said, "And besides, I think the curse happens because you take the ribbon. Ya know, covet it. Like in the bible. If you accidentally touch it, you might not even see it, so you can't be blamed for the awful things that will happen to your family."

"Thanks, cuz. That makes me feel much better. If my mom, dad, or sister get hurt or killed, I'm dead! Please don't tell anyone, Rick. Please!"

He was shaking, so I punched him in the arm and gave him a bear hug. "I got your back, cuz. No worries. Let's just leave it and go fishing. No one will know we were here."

"Thanks, Rick." We walked out of the barn and started laughing. "It's just a stupid story anyway, right?"

"Right," I replied, wondering why the hair on the back of my neck was standing, and I was shivering in the 85° humid heat of the Midwest.

∞∞∞∞

There is a creek on my grandparent's farm that houses catfish and wide mouth bass. Fred and I go fishing more to talk, but we've caught a few that were big enough to eat.

"Ya think your mom is ready to gut a fish yet?" Fred laughed because my mom is an ER nurse at Grady Hospital in Atlanta and loves to tell us explicit and disgusting stories of gunshot victims and traffic accidents that she works on but won't cut the head off a dead fish.

"Doubt it. Must be the smell. She obviously loves blood and guts."

We sat on an old log and talked about girls. Fred bragged, "Got the best blowjob ever last month. She let me come in her mouth. Felt great."

"Did you kiss her afterward?" I asked.

Fred pushed me in the water. "You're disgusting, man! Let's go. Fish aren't bitin' today."

We laughed as we walked back to the house. I never did find out if he kissed that girl.

"I'm starving. I hope lunch is ready," I said to Fred as we walked by the barn. I didn't mention the ribbon.

"Me too."

Just then we heard a loud scream coming from my grandparent's house. We looked at each other and took off running to see what had happened.

Chapter 4 -- Unexpected Tragedy

It was a female, but I couldn't tell if it was an adult or a kid.

"It's comin' from upstairs!" Fred shouted as he climbed the stairs two at a time. I was right behind him in the long, open hallway on the second floor. I was so focused on the screaming, I didn't notice that Fred stopped, and I smacked right into him. "Shit! Come on, Fred. Move."

He didn't, so I walked around him and ran to my Aunt Faith who was standing near hers and Fred's dad's bedroom door. When she saw me, she stopped screaming and pushed me so hard, I fell.

"NO! NO!" she shouted. "Don't come closer. Stay there." She closed the door and walked a few steps toward me. She put her hand out to help me up, and when I took it, it was cold and clammy.

"Aunt Faith. What's in there?" I got up and kinda pushed her towards Fred. My mom and grandma were walking down the hallway towards us.

"What happened?" asked my mom.

"I have no idea," was all I could say. My mom looked at my aunt and saw the fear in her eyes.

"Faith, honey. Why were you screaming? Is there a raccoon or something in the room? You look terrified." My mom rubbed Aunt Faith's back. She looked surprised when she felt the coldness as well.

"It's Derrick. He's. . ."

Aunt Faith saw Fred starting to move, grabbed his arm, and yanked him back to her side. "DO NOT go in that room! Do you hear me!" I saw blood dripping from Fred's arm: his mother's fingernails punctured his skin. Fred nodded and began to cry.

"I'm sorry, Ma."

"Someone has to go in there," I mouthed to my mother. Grandma looked scared for her son, and she was doing all she could to keep her composure for his family.

"What should we do?" I whispered.

187

Mom went into ER nurse mode. "Rick, Let's get grandma, Aunt Faith, and Fred downstairs. Get some water for them and wait on the back porch. Message your dad 9-1-1 and tell him he needs to get home now. I'll come back to check on Uncle Derrick."

I didn't answer. I guided Aunt Faith and Fred down the steps, my mom and Grandma right behind us. We went to the porch, and I texted my dad. Mom waited while I got the water. I sat next to Grandma on the glider, and she put her head on my shoulder. She was crying softly, still trying to stay strong. Fred and his mom were hugging and crying. I didn't know what to say.

Grandpa's 1965 red Cadillac was coming down the long dusty driveway to the house. The car stopped, and the four men got out, laughing and hitting each other. *Dad hasn't read my text.*

I started to get up to warn them, but there was no need. My mother's screams stopped them in their tracks.

Chapter 5 -- Family Get Together

Fuck! This is bad. Dad and my two uncles took off running. I shouted, "It's Uncle Derrick!" as they ran by us on the porch.

My grandfather was walking as fast as he could, and I went outside to help him. "Grandpa, it's Uncle Derrick. I'm not sure what happened, but it doesn't sound good." He likes being the caregiver, and I figured I'd prepare him, if that was possible. He took my arm and walked a little faster.

"Richard! Thank God, you're home. I don't know what's going on." Grandma walked into his open arms.

He looked at her, put his hand on her cheek, "It's okay, dear. Everything will be fine."

Aunt Faith walked over to them. She pulled them apart and slapped them on their faces. "Don't you dare say that, Richard! Don't you fuckin' dare say it's okay! My husband, your son... is dead. And he's not just dead...he's...." She began sobbing. "It's disgusting!" She sat back down next to Fred and sobbed into her hands.

"Oh God! Help us," she kept saying.

Grandpa and Grandma stood by the door, looking scared and confused. I knew better than to ask for any comfort. I had to step up right now.

"Why don't the two of you sit?" I said as I half walked/half pushed them to the glider. "Grandpa, would you like some water?" I didn't wait for an answer. I ran into the kitchen and brought him back a glass.

As I handed it to him, I said, "I'm goin' upstairs and see what's happening. Don't come up, yet. Let me talk to my mom and your sons. Okay, Grandpa? Please stay here with Grandma, Aunt Faith, and Fred. They need you." He nodded and put his free hand on my grandmother's leg. *The comforter.* I walked, slower than normal, up the stairs and down the long hallway.

∞∞∞

My mom sat on the floor outside Uncle Derrick's bedroom. Her legs were bent, and her head was down, so I couldn't see her face. "Mom? Are you alright?" I asked quietly.

She looked up and shook her head. She patted the floor next to her, and I sat down. "He committed suicide, Rick. Poor Faith." She hugged me and cried.

"Why? He never seemed depressed or anything. How did he do it?" I realized how shitty that sounded. "I mean; how do you know he killed himself?"

"He is hanging from the pull-up bar he had from high school." Uncle Derrick was a strong, healthy man. "His weight must have broken his neck. He looks contorted. And..." she paused. "His eyes were open and bulging."

"Damn! Poor Aunt Faith!"

"I know. I closed his eyes before the guys got to the room. They're taking him down and looking for a note or some sign of what happened. Don't say anything about his eyes, okay?"

"I won't. Mom, should we call the police? Or an ambulance or something?"

"I guess. But I think I should talk to Dad first. I don't want to take over. That's his brother." She cried softly.

"Could someone else have done that to him? I mean, like murder?" *I didn't want to sound dramatic, but Uncle Derrick. . . no fuckin' way!* And I kept thinkin' about the red ribbon.

"Doubtful. I've seen murder victims by hanging and strangulation, and Derrick looked different. It was almost like he calculated how far he needed to drop to break his neck. The desk chair was in front of his body on the ground. It looked planned."

"Damn!"

"I know, everyone lost a relative today...a husband, father, son, brother. So sad. You and I, Rick...we gotta hold it together for them."

"I know. I'll knock and ask if I should call someone." I stood up and stepped over my mom's feet and knocked on the bedroom door. "Dad?" I said., then added, "It's Rick. My Uncle William opened the door about six inches.

"What do you need, Ricky?" he asked. Uncle William and Uncle Derrick moved to Alaska together and were tight. I could tell he'd been crying and was shaken.

"Should I call someone? The police? Or an ambulance? Or a neighbor? I just want to help." Before he could answer, my dad opened the door wider. I couldn't see in the room because the two men blocked my view. *Thank God.*

"Rick. Thanks for wanting to help. I was thinkin' we should call someone too. But it's not a crime scene, so why call the police? I think we should call Clurkins Funeral Home. If they don't come, they should know who to call. Would you mind doing that?"

"Not at all. You good, Dad?"

"No, but we'll manage. He hugged me and closed the bedroom door.

Chapter 6 -- The Pain Continues

It turns out that I had to call the hospital to send an ambulance for the body. An autopsy had to be performed to confirm cause of death. Then Clurkins Funeral Home would receive the body for burial. So, I called the nearest hospital, William Newton Hospital in Winfield, and they said they'd dispatch an ambulance from the Udall Fire Department. I thanked the lady I spoke with and went back inside the house.

Everyone was in the living room now. The air conditioning felt much better than the sweltering heat on the porch. I knew my mom had us out there so no one would hear what was going on. My dad and the other two men had taken down Uncle Derrick's body from the pull-up bar, wrapped him in a sheet and blanket, and left him on the bed.

"Did you find a letter? Anything to tell us why?" Aunt Faith was asking my dad.

"I'm sorry, Faith. There's nothing. I have his phone if you are up to trying that. Do you know his password?"

She nodded and took the phone from my father's outstretched hand. She was shaking.

"Let me help, Faith," said my mom. "What's his password?"

"050585. Our anniversary. We had to get married on a Sunday because he was working six days a week." Faith smiled weakly at the memory.

My mom handed Faith the phone. The wallpaper was a little girl in long braids. The kitchen she was in looked like it was the 1940s or 50s. Her red velvet dress had a Peter Pan collar, and her shoes were black patent leather Mary Jane's. She was holding a Barbie-sized doll. "Do you know this little girl?"

Faith stared at the picture for a moment. "No idea. What's she holding in her hand?" I was sitting next to Aunt Faith and looked at the photo. I tensed up.

"Can I?" I asked and held out my hand. Aunt Faith gave me the phone. I touched the screen to enhance the picture. I zoomed in on the doll. My dad looked at me. We knew who it was. "Snow White," we said simultaneously.

"What?" asked Uncle Jim. "Did you say Snow White? Like in the Seven Dwarfs?"

My dad and I nodded our heads. I looked at the picture again. I already knew who it was before I saw the doll; Polly Oren was smiling. She was standing on a stool pointing at a calendar. In big red letters, the calendar said, 6th BIRTHDAY. The date was May 5, 1955, three weeks before she died.

∞∞∞∞∞

Before anyone could say that it was a picture of Precarious Polly, Fred began screaming. "It's my fault! It's all my fucking fault! Mom. I made it happen. I know I did!!"

I tried to console him, but he pushed me away. "I told you. I'm so sorry!" He got down on his knees in front of his mother, put his head on her lap, and cried. He kept apologizing and saying he didn't do it on purpose.

My dad looked at me. I knew he wanted an explanation. I said, "We went to the barn this morning. We were gonna try and set up a trick to scare the younger cousins when they heard the story. Fred jumped on a bale of hay...just for fun...and" I paused.

"What, Rick? What happened?"

"A dirty red ribbon fell from the hay and landed on the floor of the barn. We got kinda scared and left it there and went fishing. We haven't gone back to the barn yet."

"A dirty red ribbon?" asked Uncle Jim. "What the hell does that have to do with...damn it, Rick. Are you talking about that damn story your dad tells every year? What's the girl's name? The one who died in the tornado?"

"Polly," said Aunt Faith. "Precarious Polly. Do you want to see her picture?" Aunt Faith held up the phone for everyone to see. "She was born the same date as our anniversary." Then she fainted.

"Mom! What happened to her?" Fred, who was certain he brought evil to his family, backed away from his mom.

"It's okay," said my mom. "She's fainted." My mom got up and asked no one in particular to get a piece of chocolate or something sweet from the kitchen. She picked up Aunt Faith under her arms and laid her on the floor. "Richard, honey, will you elevate her legs and hold them? Let's get the blood back to the brain."

My mom stroked Faith's cheek and was talking to her. "It's okay, Faith. Wake up, girl. It's okay." Sure enough, my aunt opened her eyes and looked at my mom.

"What happened, Cindy? Did I fall?" My dad put her legs down and helped my mom sit her up against the sofa. Uncle Jim handed my mom a small bowl with some chocolate chips.

"It was all I could find," he said as he handed my mom the bowl. She winked and smiled, turned back to Faith and gave her a couple of the morsels.

"Have some sugar. It'll help." She watched my aunt eat the chocolate, then handed her the bowl and Faith ate some more. "Mmmm," she said. "Milk chocolate…not semi-sweet. That's what makes your cookies extra good, huh, Rachel?"

We all looked at my grandmother and she smiled at Faith. We chuckled and felt the tension ease a little. Faith looked at my mom and asked her to help her stand. Once she was back on the sofa, she looked at Fred and padded the space near her. "It's not your fault, Fred. The story is nothing more than that. A silly story meant to scare folks."

"Then why is her picture on Dad's phone?" Fred stared at my dad, daring him to find a logical answer to that question.

"How do you know it's Polly Oren? Lots of little girls wore their hair in braids. And how do you know it's Udall? The same picture could have been taken on May 5th anywhere. Maybe your dad wanted to show it to your mom because it's the day of their anniversary. And…how do we know if it's a real photograph or if it's been downloaded from a website and Photoshopped?"

Fred didn't answer. The front doorbell rang. It was the Udall Fire Department here to collect the body.

Chapter 7 -- Farewell Uncle Derrick

Thomas Keno, the EMT here for Uncle Derrick, knew the family. He graduated from high school with my Aunt Stephanie and was good friends with her husband. They even lived on the same block.

"Mr. and Mrs. Magnum, I am so sorry for your loss." He walked to my grandparents and leaned over to hug them. Then he sat down next to Aunt Faith.

"You're Derrick's wife, Faith?" I don't know if they'd ever met. She nodded, and Tom took her hands in his and looked down. I heard him whisper, "I'm sorry" then he put his hand on her shoulder and gave her an encouraging smile. "I'll take care of Derrick. He'll be in good hands."

Aunt Faith was quiet, but tears were streaming down her face. She sighed and put her head on Fred's shoulder.

My dad and Tom were talking quietly. He asked to see Uncle Derrick's body and determine the best way to bring him down. It was strange that my dad, the youngest of the five siblings, was the one who seemed in charge. He was calm and together as he explained the situation to Tom. Maybe it helped to stay busy rather than think about what was happening.

Less than five minutes later, my dad came down by himself and asked if anyone wanted to see Derrick before he was taken to the hospital. Aunt Faith took Fred by the hand and stepped forward. "Yes, please," she said to my father, and Fred and Aunt Faith walked side by side up the stairs. My father stayed in the living room.

"Mom. Dad. Would you like me to take you upstairs?"

"Rach?" asked my grandfather.

"I don't want to remember him like that. Not in his bedroom. But if you want me to, I'll go in with you."

My grandfather shook his head and uttered, "He was beautiful. That's how we'll remember."

Aunt Faith and Fred came downstairs. Fred's nose was bright red from crying. My Aunt Faith looked sad; however, she looked peaceful too.

"His soul has been cleansed. Fred carved a wolf paw on his arm for protection, and I put a cross over his heart. The evil will no longer pass through him." Fred held his head down.

Aunt Faith is an Aleutian Indian, and although she is Catholic, I thought it was dope that she went to her ancestry for her last visit with Uncle Derrick. I hugged Aunt Faith to let her know I supported her. Fred walked away.

Tom came downstairs and suggested that we all go back to the screened porch while he finished up. "Hey, Dad?" I said, a little louder than usual as we were walking back to the porch.

"Yes, son."

"Did Grandpa really beat the three of you golfing today?"

My dad looked at me like I was a major asshole. When he heard the squeaking of the gurney wheels, he responded, "We let him win! Right, Will? We all could have putted better today, but we choked for the old man." He looked at his father to lighten the mood and realized that wasn't happening.

"Huh?" said Uncle William. We all heard the doors to the ambulance slam. "Yeah, your dad's right. We double and triple putted to let the old man get the victory. Even Jim was in on it."

"It was for family," said Jim quietly as he watched the ambulance drive away. Tom didn't turn on the lights or the siren until he was back on route 55, headed to Winfield and William Newton Hospital.

We saw a car coming down the dirt road. It was my Aunt Stephanie, Uncle Gene, and the kids coming with the food for the BBQ. He always drove fast, and I barely could see the car with the dust flying around.

The car skidded to a halt and Aunt Stephanie jumped out. Uncle Jim was already outside, and we could hear him talking. We saw Aunt Stephanie hug him and he told Uncle Gene as he was comforting his sister-in-law. Gene, always easy-going and positive, took his wife into his arms and smiled. He held her for a long while.

My dad and uncle went out as the kids Annie, 16, Joseph, 12, and Fred's little sister, Anita, 11, got out of the car. My mom, Aunt Faith and I walked outside, and Anita ran into her mother's arms. It was time for Faith to be the comforter now.

The rest of us went back to the car and brought out bowls and casseroles. Uncle Gene took a cooler over to the fire pit, and we watched him light the already prepared wood and charcoal.

After all, it was BBQ night.

Part Two

Even More Precarious

Chapter 8 -- Another Malcolm Loss

My Uncle Derrick lost his family's and my Uncle William's family's savings gambling. Online poker is legal in Alaska, and Uncle Derrick started playing for fun which led to more gambling; sports betting, trips to Vegas his family thought were for business, and even a run-in with the Alaska State Police.

He never left a suicide note, but we figured he killed himself in his childhood bedroom because he felt safest there…it was home. And a couple thousand miles from Alaska. With no savings, no future, and no brother in Alaska, Uncle William and his family moved back to Udall to revamp and run the family farm. My Aunt Faith, Fred, and Anita moved to the Aleut reservation. No one has heard from them.

My grandfather passed away the winter after the suicide. Everyone except Uncle Derrick's family flew in for the funeral, and the Magnum family seemed lost.

My grandmother wanted Grandpa's wake to be a celebration of life. He was almost 90 years old, and she believed we should remember the happy times. I'd just turned 16 and had spent the last five months trying to make sense of what happened. Precarious Polly wasn't responsible for the sad times for the family, but I couldn't get that damn red ribbon in the barn out of my mind. I doubt that anyone had been in there since Fred and me, and I had to know.

We were all staying at the farmhouse. It was the day after my grandfather was buried, and the siblings were discussing the best plan to relocate Uncle William and his family and get the farm producing again. The other cousins were all at Aunt Stephanie's house baking cookies with Uncle Gene. It was time for a walk to the barn.

It was January in the Midwest. The snow was almost bearable, but the goddamn wind made my ears so numb I was waiting for them to freeze and fall off. *Georgia Boy Dies from Exposure*. I smiled as I thought up the headline for my obit. I would have written; *Dumbass Needs to Buy a Hat*. I put my hands over my ears and ran to the barn.

I spent a minute trying to warm up. The barn was just as cold, but the blowing snow and wind were gone. "Shit!" I said to no one.

I stood facing the barn door... Yeah, I was scared, but if I didn't look, I would wonder for the rest of my life. There was enough daylight creeping through the rotted wood that I didn't need a lantern or flashlight. I turned around with my eyes closed. When I opened them, I saw the ribbon. It was the same one from the day Fred and I saw it; dirty, long, and a little faded.

The ribbon was back on top of the bale of hay with something next to it. *Fuck!* I walked over to the bale of hay and saw an old, dirty stuffed animal.

Chapter 9 -- What Else is in There?

Someone put this here. I couldn't see any logic behind this stupid-ass message. Okay, two family members have died in less than six months, but neither of them was suspicious. Uncle Derrick's suicide sucked, but when we heard the details about the gambling, it made suicide plausible.

The thing about the picture on his phone…my dad confessed…it was downloaded and Photoshopped to look like Precarious Polly on her birthday. My dad was in on the whole thing with Uncle William. They planned to use it that Thursday night. They didn't say anything that afternoon because Aunt Faith was so upset. My dad felt like shit when Aunt Faith fainted, and he said he prayed while he was holding her legs up. I won't even go into how mad my mom was when he told the truth. He slept in the guest room for a week.

Who can I trust? Fred is the only one I know who believed that Precarious Polly could exist. I thought back to the last reunion: everyone in my family could be a suspect. But a suspect of what? When I thought about how many families in Udall said she haunted them, I got pissed cuz it was bullshit. That's when I saw the ribbon on the ground, lying near my Timberland boot.

"Fuck!" I shouted and backed up. It had to be the wind.

Except there wasn't any wind in the barn. "Is someone in here?"

"Polly?" *This is crazy.*

I heard a door slam. I turned around and saw no one. I took a breath and walked to the back of the barn. I thought about Grandpa teaching me how to use the equipment that I walked past. The John Deere tractor looked new because he washed it every time he used it. *I'm gonna miss the old guy.*

There was the culprit. The window in the loft was open, and one side of the wood shutters kept opening and closing. *That explains a few things.* I climbed the ladder, half-expecting to see a little girl sleeping on the hay and lambs' wool blankets I knew were up there.

Nothing was any different than I remembered. I closed the shutter, secured the latch with a long piece of hay. "That should do it." I climbed down the ladder and left the barn. It felt like I was invading someone's space.

I ran back to the house. The wind was blowing with me, so at least I didn't get snow on my face. I decided then to go to the library tomorrow.

When I was on the screened porch, I heard my mom say, "Where were you? It's freezing! And take off your shoes before you track in the kitchen."

"I took a walk. You were all talking adult stuff and everyone else is at Aunt Stephanie's. I kinda wanted to say good-bye to Grandpa my own way." *Part of that was true.*

"That's very sweet. You want some cocoa?"

"Definitely."

I sat at the table while my mom made the hot chocolate.

My grandmother's apron was folded on the counter laying across a cookbook. *Why does that look so creepy?* I shivered?

Mom brought our mugs over and we drank, each of us lost in our own thoughts. Suddenly, I jumped and spilled hot cocoa all over. It wasn't the apron. It was the red ties. They were laying across the cookbook just like Precarious Polly's ribbon was lying across the stuffed animal.

Chapter 10 -- A Trip to Town

"Oh God! Sorry, Mom." I jumped up to get paper towels. At least the mug didn't break.

"What's on your mind, Rick? I was watching you and you look upset."

"It's nothing. Seriously. I was thinking about last summer and Uncle Derrick, which made me think of Fred and Aunt Faith, which led me to Precarious Polly, which gave me chills. That's it."

"Precarious Polly?" asked my mom as she poured more hot chocolate for me. "Why?"

"Remember how Fred and I went to the barn and saw the red ribbon? It freaked him out. I walked past the barn just now and got spooked. It's all good now."

"Please. The last thing William and his family need to think about is Precarious Polly haunting the place. Okay?"

"I hear ya," I smiled. "I'm going to go to the Udall library in the morning to see what information I can find in the archives about the 1955 tornado. I'm doing a research project in history and thought the tornado might be an interesting subject."

"I agree. Let me know what you find out."

I nodded. We changed the subject to Grandpa and how Grandma was holding up and she forgot about Precarious Polly.

I wish I could.

∞∞∞∞

I walked to the library. It was cold but not as windy. I did wear a hat I found in the coat closet. The library opened at 10:00 and was empty except for the librarian, Bertha Rhoads, who was very helpful. She looked grateful to answer a question. School was in session, and it   didn't look like a lot of adults frequented the library.

"I'm looking for information on the tornado of 1955 that I might not find online. My family is from Udall, and we live in Georgia now, and I'm researching for a history project."

215

"That sounds quite interesting young man. I wondered why you weren't in school today. Are you Richard Magnum's grandson?" I nodded. "I'm so sorry to hear about your loss. We all loved Richard."

"Thank you, Miss Rhoads. He lived a good life. We had a celebration of life rather than a wake. It was nice. The funeral was sad, though."

"Call me, Miss Bertha, honey." She walked around the counter and put her hand on my back. "Funerals are sad events?" She smiled as we walked towards a door in the back of the room. "This is where we keep our archives. Don't get too excited about finding a lot. The biggest file is about the tornado, but it's mostly the funerals of those we lost, and how the rebuilding was going. The newspapers around Udall ran the same stories. There may be a few others from the bigger cities like Wichita. That's about it."

"You said 'we' lost, Miss Bertha. You don't look old enough to have been alive in 1955."

"How sweet you are. I was six years old, asleep in my mother's arms in the storm cellar and don't remember a thing about the tornado. I do remember afterward." She looked down at the floor.

"Would you mind if I asked you a few questions after I look through the folder? I'd love to have an interview as one of the sources for my project."

"That would be fine. I'll be at my desk." She seemed to perk up when I included her, and she walked back to the counter with a big smile on her face.

So, I'm not doing a research paper on the tornado. But the lady was the same age as Polly Oren, maybe even a friend! She had to have known her. I spent about 10 minutes taking pictures of articles with my phone. *I'll look at them later. Miss Bertha seemed like the type who would keep talking and talking if I asked the right questions.* I wanted as much of the three hours that the library was open today to be between her and me. I put away the articles and went back to the main room of the library.

"Thanks, Miss Bertha. You were right. There wasn't much new information in the archives. Do you have a few moments?"

"I do. I'm sorry, dear. I didn't get your name."

"It's Rick. Richard Magnum III. My dad is a meteorologist at the Weather Channel."

"I should have known. I see the resemblance. Your dad used to come in here for science books all the time. Besides the romance novel section, it's the biggest collection we own. Miss Holly, the librarian back then, couldn't keep enough available for your dad. He loved books!"

"You should see our house. There are books everywhere." I laughed some more. "Can we sit at a table together?" Miss Bertha nodded, grabbed a Kansas State University mug of coffee, and joined me at the oak library table nearest to her desk.

Chapter 11 -- Librarians Know Everything

"You know, Miss Bertha, I'd like you to start by telling me your story. What you remember, who your friends were, what happened to the people you knew, how you as a community survived. I'll take some notes and write some follow-up questions if I have any. I think most people who share like they're talking with a friend are much more comfortable than answering questions in a formal interview. Does that sound okay?"

"You are a wise young man, Rick." She took a sip of coffee. "Most folks who know the story of Precarious Polly ask me right away if I knew her." She looked at my eyes, and I did my best to look like I was interested because of my research. She bought it.

"Did you know my dad tells the story every year at our family reunion? I thought it was an urban legend. Maybe a rural legend."

"That's funny. Well, the story has certainly been embellished through the years, but Polly and I were best friends. When I heard that the tornado took both her parents and she was missing, I wouldn't go outside for months. My family's house was the one that wasn't touched by the tornado. I've carried that guilt for 50 years.

"I had nightmares sometimes that scared me so much, I'd vomit. The family doctor in town died in the tornado, and it took almost three weeks to clean up enough debris before we could drive to Winfield to see a doctor. There weren't therapists or psychiatrists around Udall. It was the 50s...people didn't even know that kind of help existed." Miss Bertha chuckled and wiped her nose with a tissue she had in the pocket of her cardigan. "It didn't matter. We knew what was wrong."

"What did the doctor in Winfield do for you?" I asked, trying to keep the subject about her so she'd relax.

"Not much. Told my parents to let me sleep in their room for a while. And he gave me a stuffed wolf. It was furry and kind of cute, but why a wolf, I asked him. He said he was from Alaska where wolves were protectors of the people. He told me it would keep me safe, and I slept with it until I was 11 years old.

"That's enough about me. You have questions about the tornado."

"Miss Bertha, you are the story, don't you see? You were part of a storm that destroyed the entire town. I'm honored to listen to your story."

"Well Rick, as the town was being rebuilt, my parents and I went to bed every night in our undamaged house. They discussed sheltering others but knew they could never choose who. Our house wasn't that big. The Red Cross built a tent community, and the town rebuilt the high school and the gymnasium first. By the fall, everyone had either moved away or stayed in the gym for shelter. It took almost two years to re-build for folks to have a home."

"Was the Oren's home completely destroyed?"

"No, the roof blew off the house; Mr. and Mrs. Oren were hit by debris in the tornado. Luckily, nothing on the first floor was damaged, so the city re-roofed it and another family moved in." She stopped talking and crinkled her forehead. "Come to think about it, the family was the doctor I went to see in Winfield. Dr. Wolfe. He had a wife and three teenagers. He accepted the job as the town's family doctor and moved here in early '56. I forgot all about that."

"What happened to him? And did you say his name was Wolf, like the stuffed animal?

"My Lord! It was spelled with an E at the end, and I never made the connection between his name and the stuffed toy! Can't say what happened to them." I went to Kansas State for college and by the time I moved back, they were gone. I think one of the boys overdosed on heroin. The 60s were crazy years…drugs, the war…"

"Did the story about Polly begin then, Miss Bertha?"

"I think. The whole country was changing. I was away at college, but I remember that a few strange deaths happened in Udall. The doctor's son had the overdose, and there were two suicides. That's when the tale started. First, it was Polly trying to hurt people because she never received a proper burial. Then, a red ribbon was found at one scene, and I think the story of the red ribbon she wore at night got added to the tale. I stopped listening after a while; it was nonsense. My friend died, and her body was never recovered. End of story."

"Miss Bertha, you said there were two suicides. How, if you don't mind me asking, did they die?"

"They both hanged themselves."

Chapter 12 -- Surmising

That's how Uncle Derrick died. Could there be a connection? "Miss Bertha, did you know my Uncle Derrick?"

"I did. His death was such a tragedy. And it surprised everyone. He never seemed sad a day in his life."

"You've shared so much with me, I guess I can tell you." I paused, and Miss Bertha leaned in a bit. "He had serious gambling debts, and we believe he was murdered because of them."

"My Lord! Murdered? No wonder Faith and the children went back to the reservation. Is there an investigation? I haven't heard a word."

"That doesn't surprise me. Everyone still thinks he committed suicide. It's more a family theory based on what we learned after his death."

"Wow! It's hard to fathom a murder in Udall, Kansas," Miss Bertha was shaking. "What happened? Can you share?"

"Well, he spent his family's retirement funds gambling. And a neighbor of Uncle William's told us a black SUV was at his house once a month. And this is kind of gross, the family dogs, two Mastiffs, were sent through a woodchipper. That was a few years ago, and Uncle William said Uncle Derrick told him the dogs ran away."

"How strange. You know, Dr. Wolfe, the one who gave me the stuffed animal, told me to watch out for angry people, you know, since we were the only ones whose house wasn't destroyed. And he also asked my dad if we had a woodchipper? I remember that because it was so strange?"

"Why do you think he would ask that? What does a woodchipper have to do with people in town being upset that your house was okay?" "Well, Dr. Wolfe grew up on the same Aleutian reservation where your Aunt Faith was raised. He was much older. Anyway, his father was from Russia, and my mom told me some wild stories about the family."

"Like?"

"Well, for one thing, he bragged about the Russian Mafia paying his way for college and that's why his family was in the Midwest...because he had to repay his debt to the people who sent him to college."

"That freaky."

"I thought so too, so I did some research. It turns out that one of the Russian Mob's signature tortures is to send people, alive, through a woodchipper! And he told me to be careful, and I was barely six. Isn't that creepy?"

"And you think that's what happened to the Mastiffs? Wow! The Russian Mafia in Alaska seems plausible since it's geographically so close. But in Udall, Kansas? That's crazy."

"Rick, sometimes I get ideas in my head that are bizarre. This might be one of them." She smiled and squinted.

"Now I'm speaking based on opinions and stories, Rick. I don't want you to worry about your family. I would feel terrible if I did that. My job leaves me lots of time to think. I've concocted some wild stories!" She laughed.

"I like to approach a problem from every angle. I think you do the same, with some drama added for effect." I smiled at her and stood. "Miss Bertha, you have been very helpful, and I appreciate our conversation. I think I should get back to the farmhouse before they wonder what happened to me."

"I'm surprised that your Aunt Stephanie never mentioned the suspicion of murder to me. We're good friends."

"Well, some of the family have a hard time talking about Uncle Derrick. She was pretty shaken up."

We shook hands and Miss Bertha grabbed me and gave me a tight hug. I heard her sniffle and wondered why she would be crying. I patted her back until she released her grip. "Thank you for letting me reminisce, Rick." I smiled and left the library.

∞∞∞

The sun was shining, and I enjoyed the walk back to the farmhouse, despite the cold. Ninety minutes with Miss Bertha didn't really give me anything good about Precarious Polly, but she did make me wonder if the stuffed animal in the barn was a wolf. I had to decide if I was curious enough to go back in. *Damn! I wish Fred were here.* The stories she had. I don't think she picked up that I'm the only Magnum who thinks Uncle Derrick was murdered by the Russian Mafia! I laughed out loud.

Uncle Gene stopped and picked me up on the dirt road. I smelled the cookies when I got in. "God, I'm starving." I hadn't eaten anything yet.

"Good because we are having lunch soon. There is so much food from neighbors and friends, grandma has enough for months!"

He wasn't exaggerating. I saw whole hams, a dozen Pyrex casseroles, huge fruit baskets, salads, desserts. It filled the screened porch. Uncle Gene and my cousins and I washed our hands in the kitchen sink and sat at the dining room table.

My grandmother tapped her water glass with her spoon to quiet us. "Before we begin eating, I wanted to say thank you to everyone for celebrating Richard's life rather than mourning his loss. I know we've been through hell in the last six months, but it didn't seem right to be somber about someone who brought such joy to our lives." She smiled even though tears were streaming down her face. "I am going to miss him so much."

My dad stood to hug her. "It was a beautiful service, Mom, and we get to remember the love Dad gave us. We need to thank you." She wiped her eyes and shooed Dad away, telling us that we had better be hungry because what was on the table wasn't half of what was brought. That brought a smile to her face. I knew she was thinking how well-liked Grandpa was.

I thought about what I'd learned today, about Uncle Derrick, not about Precarious Polly. I don't remember anyone bringing food when he passed. Aunt Faith also insisted that his body be returned to Alaska and cremated. My grandmother was upset but had no choice. She was adamant.

We never talked much about Uncle Derrick's death until Gramps passed and we flew to Kansas. I know my dad talked to Grandma almost every day, and I knew he missed his brother, but I had no idea how to talk to him about grieving or stuff like that. I'd hear him talk to Grandma or Uncle William, but I never asked for details. I decided to wait until we got home and ask him about what Miss Bertha told me.

Chapter 13 -- Let it Go

My father and I flew back to Georgia the next day. He didn't want me to miss more school, and he couldn't be gone from work any longer. Grandma had agreed to come to Suwanee and stay with us until the Spring or Summer. My dad convinced her that Uncle William needed to settle in and get the farm back to a working condition. I know he didn't want her to stay there any longer without her husband. My mom and she would be driving to Georgia in Grandma's Volvo in the next week or two.

Since it only was us on the flight home, I asked him about Miss Bertha and all she shared. "Please, Rick, hasn't there been enough craziness for our family? Hell, for the whole town of Udall. There's no need to create another outlandish story about crazy people in town. I mean, people die, sometimes by their own hands, but there's no Precarious Polly haunting the citizens of Udall, and I guarantee there is no Russian Mafia killing its residents. Bertha Rhoads is a little wacko anyway."

"I thought she was nice. She seemed normal to me."

"Well, after what happened to her family, it's amazing that she can talk about death without losing it."

"Because their house was the only one that wasn't damaged?"

"No, her husband and son. They were killed when their boat caught fire on a trip down the Mississippi. I think they were going to visit his family in Louisiana, and Bertha gets seasick, so she flew to New Orleans. They never made it. Things were so burnt up; they never did determine what caused the explosion. Happened in the 90s. I guess you were too young to remember. Sad."

"She didn't say anything about it. Do you think her family's death had anything to do with Dr. Wolfe?"

"Rick, where are you getting these ideas? There are no gangsters, no mob connections in Udall, Kansas. The worst thing that's happened there besides the tornado is that the bowling alley filed bankruptcy. Bad things happen everywhere, son. So, there have been a few strange deaths in town, but nothing that involved organized criminal activity. Unless the Russian mob is putting corn on the black market." He laughed again and smacked my leg. "Let it go. Okay?"

"I will. But it doesn't explain Precarious Polly, why three people committed suicide by hanging themselves, and why those red ribbons keep showing up unexpectedly. I think there should be a logical explanation."

"Well, son, I will be predicting the weather tomorrow for the country. With the technology, the science, and how much more we know about weather patterns, tornados, hurricanes, tsunamis and Mother Nature still will kill people every year. Not knowing is frustrating, but all we can do is to keep learning and keep trying to improve."

I nodded my head, knowing he was done listening. My mind was filled with red ribbons and woodchippers.

Part Three

Not in the Heart of the Midwest

Chapter 14 -- College, Career, and Continued Curiosity

Life continued. I graduated from Suwanee High School and was accepted to the University of Washington in Seattle. I planned to study electrical engineering, and I got a great financial aid package. Mostly, I wanted to be somewhere not the South or the Midwest, and Stanford and the University of California both declined my application, so UDub and Seattle it was.

I love Seattle, the whole Pacific Northwest, actually; however, I hated engineering. I ended up getting my bachelor's degree in law & justice, a steppingstone to my master's program in criminal science investigation. I loved getting my hands dirty and eking out the truth. I'm good at researching, and when I joined the Seattle Police Department, I became known for finding the clues that weren't possible to find. If you look at enough data, it will solve the crime or will lead you in the right direction. Even though I ended up with a desk job, I still love CSI work over engineering by far.

My parents retired and moved to Sammamish, WA, on the outskirts of Seattle. I got married to a beautiful woman who works as a sketch artist for SPD. We love the Northwest. It's been a good life.

My grandmother passed less than a year after my grandfather, Uncle William sold the family farm and moved to Austin, Texas, where he and my Uncle Jim went into business together buying old houses, fixing them up, and selling them for profit. He didn't have the farmer in him, even though he loves hands-on work. Personally, I think he hated Udall, but I never brought it up.

The family reunion became a yearly trip to Las Vegas, and as the family grew and technology made it easy to keep in touch, that faded away as well.

My wife, Katherine, and I were having dinner at the Space Needle with my parents when I mentioned Udall, and I asked them if anyone had been there lately. Even my Aunt Stephanie and Uncle Gene moved to Poland, Ohio, Uncle Gene's hometown, after the kids married and left. The Magnum family name wasn't even in the Udall telephone directory anymore. "I wonder if the Precarious Polly story is still alive and well?"

"Rick, I know you're good at your work, but please don't bring up that stupid story again," said Katherine. "I am so tired of your theories and predictions about what really happened. Mom, Dad, did he ever tell you he thought the Russian Mafia killed people in Udall?"

"No," said my mom. "I never heard that one. Have you?" she asked my dad.

"We talked about it once, on the plane ride back to Georgia after Dad passed. I told him the same thing as you, Katherine. Let it go."

We all laughed, although the researcher in me wanted to know the truth. A waiter came over to the table. "Excuse me for interrupting, but I heard you mention Udall, Kansas. My father grew up there."

"Wow, what a small world," said my mom. What's your name?"

"Jeremiah Wolfe. My grandfather was the town doctor."

Chapter 15 -- Finding the Truth

My parents had no reaction to the waiter's name. "I don't remember the name," said my dad. "When did he practice in Udall?"

"In the late 50s and the 60s. I think the town doctor before him got killed in a tornado. Do you remember that?"

"None of us was born, but we all know about the tornado," my dad replied.

"I was born and raised in Seattle, so I don't know much about life in small towns. My grandfather rarely talked about it. The family moved back to Alaska after one of his sons died from a drug overdose in the 60s. I don't think he liked thinking about it."

"Sorry to hear about your...great Uncle," I said, trying to keep the conversation going. *If you research enough, you'll find what you need to solve the crime.* "Is your grandfather still living?"

"He passed away when I was a kid. He and my grandmother were killed in an automobile accident. They drove off a cliff on a winding road just outside of Nome, Alaska. They had to use dental records to identify their bodies. Even the FBI was surprised that there was nothing left. I can't remember it too much, but dad does."

"Is it possible to talk with him?" I asked.

"Rick!" Katherine kicked me in the shin. *Ouch.* I didn't show a reaction.

"Sorry, Jeremiah. I work CSI for the Seattle PD and get carried away."

"No problem. My dad is in his late 70s and is retired, but I think he would love to talk to someone about those days. "Would you excuse me for a moment?" He went back to his customers.

"Rick, I'm done with this Precarious Polly shit. You know how pissed off I get." My wife's face was flushed. She had her own skeletons and didn't like to talk about the past.

"KAM (Katherine Ann Magnum), you know how long I've been trying to get a lead. What if the kid's dad knows something we don't? And you heard him say that the doctor and his wife were burned beyond recognition? What does that remind you of...Bertha Rhode's husband and son! What if their deaths are related?"

"Right. A couple in Alaska drives off a cliff, and you think it's related to a boat fire on the Mississippi River more than 40 years ago? Richard, Cindy...has he always been this obsessive?"

"Yes," they both said at the same time. "I'm sure it's why he opted for the Dick Tracey job instead of engineering," added my mom. She smiled.

"You know I hated it. And both of us love our jobs and the city. Right, KAM?"

"Yeah, it's great. Everything except for this Precarious Polly nonsense."

Jeremiah Wolfe came back to our table and handed me a card with his father's name and email address. "He lives on Bainbridge Island now."

"Thanks, Jeremiah. My name is Richard Magnum. I'll get in touch with your dad soon. I appreciate this very much."

"It's cool, Mr. Magnum. I'm sure he'll enjoy the company."

As we rode the elevator back to the street level, I took Katherine's hand and kissed it. "Thank you," I whispered, knowing she would be supportive as I pursued this new lead in the Precarious Polly case.

Chapter 16 -- The Truth About Precarious Polly

Bainbridge Island is a 35-minute ferry ride from Seattle across Puget Sound. I walked from the station and sat on the main deck for the ride. It was easy contacting Mr. Wolfe (Robert) and setting up a meeting. He lived in a condo less than a quarter of a mile from the ferry terminal on Bainbridge, so I got there with time to spare.

I've gone over the Precarious Polly story so many times I didn't bring any notes or questions with me. I remembered when I "interviewed" Bertha Rhoads when I was in high school. I let her do the talking and that got her telling me more than I even knew to ask. Jeremiah said Robert might enjoy reminiscing. *Let's hope he's in the mood today.*

I buzzed Mr. Wolfe's condo, 5B, and I heard the lock on the door open. I took the elevator to the top floor. He was at his door waiting. "Mr. Magnum? Or is it Detective?" He held out his hand and firmly shook mine.

"Rick is fine. May I call you Robert?" I was trying to get him to relax, even though he already looked pretty content to me.

"Sure, Rick. It's funny how I never shortened my name to Bob or Robbie. Is your first name Richard?"

"Richard Magnum III. My mom called me Rick because she despised people calling me little Richard. I was fine with Rick. It's stuck all these years."

"Little Richard. That's funny!" Robert smiled. "But I know you aren't here to talk about your name." The smile left his face.

"I've been trying to understand the story of Precarious Polly since I was in high school. Do you remember hearing about her?"

"I do."

"From what I've learned, it appears that Polly Oren somehow became the center of a tall tale that grew due to several strange occurrences in Udall, Kansas. There were two suicides after the tornado. The first man used a red ribbon and hanged himself. The fall broke his neck. Then, a few years later, another male hanged himself with a rope. His fall took his head right off. The body was under the rope, and the head rolled down a small hill. There was a dirty red ribbon next to it."

"I knew about those two men. They died when we lived in Udall. My father determined cause of death for both: suicide by hanging. I saw the headless body. It still haunts my dreams." Robert looked out the window watching a ferry dock.

"How did you see the bodies?" I wondered why his father would let a kid see that kind of gore.

"I'd go to his office after school sometimes. It was in the center of town, right down the street from the high school."

"I've seen a lot working for the Seattle P.D.! But a headless body isn't one of them. Have you been back to Udall since your family left?"

"No. I enjoy the quiet life now, but I hated it as a teenager. Cornfields, hayrides, and church on Sundays. How boring. But it's where we were sent, and you don't get much choice in the matter."

"Where who sent you?"

Chapter 17 -- Learning the Truth

Robert looked at me for almost a minute. He knew why I was there, and I knew he was deciding exactly what and how much to say. We sized each other up. Finally, he said, "I know you can't do anything regarding the law, Rick. You have no jurisdiction outside Seattle. We took the chance that you might not end up as an engineer when we sent you to the Pacific Northwest, but the CSI route had us on edge for a while. You lack ambition though, so my sister and I decided to let you live out your days in peace."

"Excuse me." I felt uncomfortable and my palms were sweaty. Suddenly, this sweet old man got creepy. "I don't appreciate your comment about my lack of ambition. I have one of the finest resolution rates the SPD has ever seen."

"Well, it's Seattle, Rick. What happens around here? A protest march in Pioneer Square or Jeff Bezos has some foreign hackers downloading eBooks from Amazon for free? Christ, nothing happens around here." He sat up in his chair and looked a lot stronger than I first thought. The look in his eyes made me glad I had my gun.

"Robert, I'm not sure how our conversation turned like it has. I have no idea how your family could be involved with mine. I asked my father if Dr. Wolfe was his pediatrician, and he said they went to the family doctor in Winfield. That's where my grandmother was born."

"You're right, Rick. Your family, along with the rest of the town, never suspected a doctor would be a killer or would teach his children how to cover their tracks." He looked at me and squinted his eyes. "I can see the resemblance to Derrick Malcolm a bit. But your dad was the college boy, and he raised you to be fair-minded and studious…wimpy. Derrick lived in Alaska, was blue-collar, pipeline tough. He really fucked himself."

"You knew my uncle. How?"

"Rick, I'm an old man. I don't give a damn about my future, long or short. But if I answer your questions, I need to know that Jeremiah won't find out."

"I'm pretty sure you're about to answer some questions that have haunted me for years. I'm good at finding answers, and if what you are about to tell me involves illegal activity, I can't guarantee that I won't repeat it. I give you my word though that Jeremiah will be safe."

"How bad do you want to know, Rick? I'm finished speaking until I feel in my gut, you're gonna keep this here. I can tell you why Polly Oren became Precarious Polly, why your uncle and two other males were murdered, and they looked like suicides. I can tell you why Bertha Rhoads' husband and son were killed, why my own parents were killed. I'll even explain why someone visited your uncle every month and put his dogs through a woodchipper. I know you're good at finding answers, but you've been searching for these answers for years and haven't gotten very far. How frustrating."

"Yes, it is. And how my uncle's death, the others' deaths, and Precarious Polly are connected is the newest question I have about this shit. Give me a moment to think."

"No problem." He got up and said he needed to take a piss.

Chapter 18 -- A Tale of Turmoil

Fuck! As Robert walked down the hall to the bathroom, I asked myself what the hell I'd gotten into. Torture and kill? That shit doesn't happen in Seattle much; Robert was right. But in Udall, Kansas? No way! I have this feeling that no matter what I answer, he is gonna be trouble. *Damn*! I heard him coming back to the living room.

"So, what's it going to be, Rick? The truth or good-bye?"

"Do I have a choice?"

"Of course. We all have a choice. It is disappointing, though, when there are no good ones."

"This isn't going to end well, is it Mr. Wolfe?"

"It's Volkov, actually. That translates to wolf in English. Thus, our American surname."

"You are Russian?"

"Dah (yes)," he said. "What's it gonna be, Rick. Time is precious at my age." He looked at me with no expression.

"My only choice is to listen. May I ask questions?"

"When I am finished speaking."

"Fine." I crossed my leg and tried to look relaxed. I felt my heart pounding though. I took a deep breath.

"Relax, Rick, sometimes I try to sound like a hard-ass. It's a hard habit to break. Your family business has been resolved, so my threats are merely for show." He smiled. I did not.

"My grandfather, Victor Volkov, was exiled from Russia in the early 1900s as the Soviet Union and the communist party were gaining power. He was thrown overboard from a cargo ship and swam nearly two miles to reach the shore. He landed on an Aleut tribe island and became a welcomed guest. Many ancestors of the Aleuts were of Russian blood. That is where he met his wife, Marie Lydia, and they had seven children. My father was their youngest, and when he came of age begged his parents to send him to college to become a doctor.

"Since his parents had no money, Marie Lydia convinced her husband to return to Russia and ask his relatives for help. The Soviet Union had become very powerful, and the Volkov name was known by many. Our history is well-known in many places, even today. My grandfather returned to the land we now call Chechnya, where many of our relatives still reside. Despite the turmoil between the Red Army and Southern Russia, the Volkov name remained strong and powerful. For my grandfather, there was only one way to gain their acceptance and trust.

"The family gave Victor the funds to send my grandfather to Harvard University and then to St. Petersburg State University for medical school."

"How did Victor gain their trust?" *I knew there was a connection!*

"First, he had to prove himself as an honorable and trusted member of the family. He spent a year in Russia working in the family business. He served them well, and they sent his son to Harvard. However, before he was permitted to go to Russian university for medical school, he also spent six months with the family and "learned the ropes." Then, the Volkov's sent him to become a doctor. And finally, they would decide where my father lived. That is how we ended up in a shithole place like Kansas?"

"It wasn't that bad."

"Not as bad as his other siblings. One had to work at a steel mill in Ohio. My grandfather returned to Alaska in the1940s and lived out his life on the Aleut reservation. His first wife passed in the late 50s, and he married another tribal member in 1962. They had only one child. A daughter named Kanuux̂ which translates to heart in English. Most of the tribe called her Faith."

My heart began pounding again. "Faith, as in Derrick's wife, Faith?"

Chapter 19 -- They Were in Udall Afterall

"Correct. The Volkov family was expanding its business in the United States, and when Faith came of age, she was sent to Fairbanks to find a suitable mate to join the family; she met your Uncle Derrick. That he was from Udall, Kansas was only a coincidence and is still fucking amazing to me. He got himself into trouble gambling, which was overlooked, but the women were unacceptable to the family. He was married to a special person. We were sent to eliminate him."

"So, my uncle was murdered by the Russian Mafia?"

"Careful, Rick. The Volkov family does not use the term mafia; we've earned a greater respect."

"I apologize."

"My father was sent to Wichita, Kansas, where my brother, sister, and I were born. He practiced in Winfield until that damn tornado, when they told my dad move to the house where that girl lived. Polly. The one this is all about. The story was that she would be the one responsible for the strange happenings if anyone ever got curious. And in a small town like Udall, it was easy to make the story more and more ominous as the years went by.

"My father had to eliminate anyone the family asked. That's why he'd make jokes about paying his debt back. He learned to predict weight and velocity, so hanging was usually his first choice. The one whose head fell off wasn't his best but planting the red ribbon at the scene was ingenious. My idea, by the way. We found dozens of red ribbons in the house we moved to; it turned out to be a great calling card."

"What did these men do to deserve to die?"

"Whatever didn't please the family. Bertha Rhoads was a nice lady who worked as a nanny for my cousins when she was in college. When my Uncle Igor found out that her husband smacked her around, he set up the explosion on the river."

"But she lost her son as well!"

"No, she was released from the evilness that her husband's genes had created. We take no chances."

"And your brother. Was he murdered too?"

"No. The asshole died from an overdose. It devastated my parents so much, they moved back to Alaska against the family's wishes. There was no accident on that highway. The Volkov family was betrayed...just another job."

We both sat quietly for a few moments, sizing each other up and deciding what to say next. I asked, "What's your role in the family?"

"No comment," Robert responded. "In case you try something stupid. Let's just say that my sister and I were given permission to move to Seattle after my parent's 'accident' and we have both been called upon several times through the years. The family doesn't know about Jeremiah. I never married because I refuse to subject my children to this lifestyle. I have friends who keep an eye on him, but it's not enough. Look what happened in a town with less than 1000 residents. They've got hundreds of eyes in Seattle. I'm always afraid." Robert looked out the window again.

I was somewhere between wanting to cuff him or pat him on the back and let him know this wasn't his fault. *Damn!*

Maybe I don't have any ambitions and let all this shit fly over my head. Seattle has its issues, but there isn't much in the way of organized crime. I needed to process this; think my way...do some research.

Chapter 20 -- Precarious Polly for a Deal

"Why did you tell me this, Robert? You know as well as I that many of the crimes you told me about have no statute of limitations. I could arrest you right now." I sat up, feeling more confident about myself. I'm talking to an old man. Maybe he was a bad man once, but I knew I could take him if I had to.

"Because I'm an old man and can't do it alone anymore. Sure, my sister's here, too, but she's in her 70s too. I want Jeremiah to be safe. Happy. Unaware."

"And why should I be the one to help you? You murdered my uncle. Don't get me wrong. If he did cheat on Aunt Faith, he deserved to be punished. But not disfigured for her to see."

"It's how the family does business, Rick. The dogs went through the woodchipper as a warning to Derrick that his family could be next, but the asshole didn't care. Sorry to disrespect the dead."

"So, your family hangs people, shreds them in woodchippers to show what? That they were responsible? That is the Volkov calling card?"

"We have no need for calling card. We follow the Russian way."

"I can't believe I'm saying this to you...how can I trust you?"

"Faith."

"I'm not a very religious man."

"I'm talking about your aunt. She went back to the reservation after Derrick died and was told everything by the tribal elders. She stayed away to protect her husband's family. She gave up her life for the Malcolm family."

"Is she still alive? Does she live on the reservation? What about Fred and Anita? I doubt they wanted to be there?"

"Slow down. One question at a time. Faith still lives in Alaska, but in Nome, not on the reservation. The family took care of the children. I believe they both live in Europe now. We lost contact years ago. The family let it go. They didn't do anything wrong."

"You've given me a lot to consider. A lot to process. I'm sure you trust me about as much as I do you. Still, I respect you and swear that I will not disclose this conversation to anyone until I talk to you first. I can't give you an answer right now because I'm not ready to decide how to feel about this whole thing. I like you, Robert. I believe you got into a situation, not by your choosing. Regardless, I'm a man of the law; I think you can understand my dilemma."

"I do. More than you know. We've been watching you most of your life. Hell, I'm a little jealous sometimes. Mind you, I'll never admit I said that." He smiled for the first time in an hour.

We both stood up and shook hands. He put his left hand on my forearm; a sign of respect, I believe. Neither of us spoke again. Both our minds were full enough.

Chapter 21 -- Another Malcom Loss

The ferry was pulling in as I walked back to the terminal. *Now I know all about Precarious Polly. And there really were mobsters in Udall. My questions have been answered, so why do I feel so shitty?* I like Robert Wolfe/Volkov. That's why I'm so pissed. I went to the top deck and stood outside. It was sunny and 70, but the wind off the sound keeps most passengers inside the ferry. I needed to be alone. I needed to think.

The horn sounded as we left the dock. The wind didn't pick up until the captain turned the ferry towards Seattle. By the time we were in the middle of the sound, I was cold, and the wind was so loud, I didn't hear the people behind me. I was standing on the side of the boat, looking at the water. I jumped when I felt a hand touch my shoulder. I immediately went for my gun.

"Hey cuz, how's it goin'?" My cousin Fred, a little wider and a little balder but still Fred was standing behind me. I left my gun in the holster and hugged him.

"Shit! What the hell are you doing here, man? It's been forever. You look great. How are you?" I pulled back and noticed a woman standing by his side. "Anita?" She smiled. "You are supposed to be a gangly 11-year-old. You're all grown up!" I hugged her as well.

"How are you? I heard you lived in Europe." When I looked at Fred and saw the look in his eyes, I didn't need an answer. We stared at each other knowing that the truth would be told.

"Robert Wolfe set me up, didn't he?" No reaction from either of them. "And I bet Jeremiah Wolfe isn't even Robert's son. Damn! Why didn't you find me sooner? Fred? Anita? Talk to me. Please."

"Robert Wolfe is our uncle. He told you about his father's last child, Kanuux̂, our mother. Uncle Robert came to visit us about a year after Derrick Malcolm died. He told us everything. He told us he would take care of us. Then, my mother tried to stab him, called him a liar, a criminal, a beast. She kept calling him Derrick. They put her in a psychiatric hospital where she's been since. Uncle Robert sent us to relatives in France, where we finished school and "learned the ropes."

"Why would you get involved with that, Fred? Why would you let Anita be subjected to that life?"

Anita spoke for the first time. "Fred didn't subject me to anything. I make my own choices. Our father, your uncle, was the true villain and we know our mother lost her mind because of his evilness."

"Why didn't you try to find us sooner? I'm sure I was easy to find. I'm sorry about what happened."

"So are we," they said in unison as they picked me up and tossed me into the cold waters of the Puget Sound. I fought but the wake from the ferry was so strong, it was useless. I held my breath and thought about Katherine, my parents, my family. Then I saw a fish swim by. It reminded me of the creek in Udall. As the water filled my lungs, I saw a beautiful little girl with a red ribbon in her long-braided hair, holding out her arms.

I'm coming, Polly. I'm coming.

The End